MURDER
on
MARTHA'S VINEYARD

Kelley Roos

WALKER AND COMPANY ✸ NEW YORK

First published in the United States of America in 1981 by the Walker Publishing Company, Inc.

Published simultaneously in Canada by Beaverbooks, Limited, Don Mills, Ontario.

ISBN: 0-8027-5436-8

Library of Congress Catalog Card Number: 80-54480

Book Design by Marjorie E. Reed

Printed in the United States of America

10 9 8 7 6 5 4 3

CHAPTER ONE

*T*HE ISLAND FERRY churned into the slip, gleaming white in the late autumn sunshine. The man on the dock, half hidden by a stack of waiting cargo, had watched it since it had steamed into view. The day was too cold, the wind too raw and rowdy for many passengers to brave the deck but he had seen the young couple standing together, leaning against the railing, before the boat had landed.

Two months ago the man on the dock had heard they were to be married. In the island paper he had read about their wedding, their honeymoon abroad. Word had spread rapidly through the town that the young couple were coming back to the island to live. She hoped, the bride was quoted as saying, for the rest of her life.

As the deckhands, bright figures in their scarlet uniforms, were securing the ferry, the foot passengers trudged ashore, struggling with their luggage. The cars followed them off. The man on the dock saw the bride sitting beside her husband in a small red sports car. She was as beautiful as he remembered her, this young bride who hoped to spend the rest of her life on the island.

Her wish would come true, he would see to that. In a few weeks or so, at his convenience, she would be dead. But she would have gotten her wish; she would have spent the rest of her life on the island.

In the town of Oak Bluffs, when the red Mercedes passed the oldest merry-go-round still in operation in the country, the young couple looked at each other and laughed. There, when she was eight and he ten, girl had met boy.

"Confidentially," David said, "what was it about me that first attracted you? The brass ring that I snatched and gave you?"

"It wasn't brass," Nancy said. "More like tin."

"But you wore it proudly."

"All that summer. And when I lost it in the sand on Labor Day, I cried all that fall."

They left the gingerbread cottages behind, drove the long stretch of road between Nantucket Sound and Sengekontacket Pond, past autumn-browned beaches splotched with crimson patches of sumac and ivy, veering around shells dropped on the pavement by squadrons of swooping seagulls, and in a few minutes they were in Edgartown, where so many of their childhood summers had been spent.

It was mid-November and the town was quiet, hotels and restaurants closed for the winter, streets almost deserted. Nearly half the houses were vacant, their shutters drawn, their window boxes, bright with ageratum and red and coral geranium in summer, were empty now. A summer town, hibernating cozily until June, when it would teem with life again.

"I think," David said softly, as though he were afraid he might scare something away, "I think at last I have an idea for the new book."

"I'm not surprised," Nancy said. "Did seeing the island do it for you?"

David laughed. Matter of fact, it did hit me on the ferry."

"Tell me?" Nancy said.

"Tonight at cocktails. It's a somewhat drastic idea. I'm wondering if I shouldn't go to New York and talk to some editors about it."

"Do that," Nancy said. "But just one editor and hurry right back."

Then she noticed that David had turned off Main Street and onto a side road. She looked at him inquiringly.

"I thought we'd drive past the Browns," he said. "Maybe Jane and Clark are up for the weekend."

"All right," Nancy said. "That's a good idea."

She knew for certain that the Browns would not be in town, that their place would be closed for the winter. David knew it, too, and she was grateful to him for the pretense. This way they would not have to pass the house on Cooke Street. Someday soon she'd be able to walk past it, to stop and look at it, remember the happy times she had had there and forget the rest. But not yet, not on her first day back on the island.

They drove past the Browns' tidy closed and shuttered cottage, and David said, "No go. No Browns. Damn."

"Maybe," Nancy said, playing the game "Browns at Thanksgiving."

"That," David said, "will be something to give thanks for."

Two blocks more, and then, on a corner facing the water was the Webster house, standing proud as a dowager in the golden afternoon light.

It had been built by a whaling captain named Lorenzo Tedrow in the 1850's. David's grandfather had bought it

7

from Captain Tedrow's aging spinster daughter in the twenties. David's father and his two sisters, and then David and *his* sister had spent all their summers when they were growing up in this house on the island. All of them loved it dearly.

It was a Greek-revival with twin portal columns—a spacious house, built when carpenters worked artistically and enthusiastically for a dollar a day. Originally it had been a house of many small rooms, each one heated by a handsome Franklin stove. The only renovating that David's grandfather, and later, his father, had done was to knock down walls, making large rooms out of small ones, replace the stove with fireplaces, remodel the kitchen, and install a few baths. But the old wide floor boards were still there, and the fanlight over the door still held its original Sandwich glass. Even the Tedrow family's privy was still there, part of a tool shed now. It was a two-holer, one of the holes a small one with steps up to it for the whaling captain's daughter when she was a little girl.

David's father had bought the land across the street and built a boathouse on the Edgartown harbor, with a dock for their sailing boats and, eventually, inevitably, the stinkpot outboard motors. The boathouse had interfered with the view of the harbor, and of the Vineyard's sister island, Chappaquiddick, but not enough to matter.

Dave stopped the car in front of the house.

"Hey, Dave, there's Mrs. Mac at the window! Hey, Mrs. Mac!" Nancy yelled, waving fiercely.

Sabra MacWilliams, island-born, aged sixty-six, a long-time widow, waved back from the window, her enthusiasm equaling Nancy's. She had been the Websters' island housekeeper for all of David's life. She hadn't seen David since before his marriage, nor Nancy since the court trial that had ended almost three years ago.

Sabra hurried to the door and flung it open. Anxiously she examined Nancy, and was delighted by what she saw. The old tomboy was back again, taking the steps to the porch in a single leap, streaked blonde hair tangled by the wind, brown eyes dancing, wide mouth stretched wider in the old impish grin. Sabra remembered the last time she had seen her, gaunt and pale and wounded, in the courthouse at Barnstable, on trial for the murder of her first husband, Jim Barrow. Silently Sabra thanked God that Nancy had come through and become herself again. Yes, she thought, Nancy had courage, and she was going to need it if she and David were to make a life for themselves here on the island.

"Welcome home," she said, hugging Nancy to her with one arm, David with the other. "Welcome home, both of you!"

It was almost ten o'clock that night, too dark and foggy for him to be seen; but still he huddled in the shadows of the boathouse, his jacket collar turned up against the dampness, watching the house across the street. He had been there for almost an hour now, staring at them through the windows. They were having drinks, and he could see that all of them were talking and smiling and laughing a lot. They were having a party. It was a party to welcome David Webster and his new wife back to the island, and the unfairness of it almost brought tears to his eyes.

Not that he had ever had anything against David Webster. David was all right. It was Nancy Ryan who had been wicked, who had told lies and done bad things, and she had escaped her punishment. Three

9

years ago she had been tried for murder and driven from the island in disgrace. Yet here she was, back again, as free as a bird, as though nothing had happened. Well, he thought grimly, all that would change soon enough. He would see to that.

The guests were getting ready to leave, setting down their glasses, putting on their coats and scarves, moving toward the center hall. The man shrank further into the boathouse shadows as the front door opened and they came out onto the porch. They stood there for a few minutes, beside the tall white columns, shaking hands and saying good-bye. Then Mickey Jamison and her husband started walking toward their house on School Street, and the Clarks, who lived on the other side of town, got in their car and drove off.

The porch was empty now. David and his wife had gone back into the house. He could see them in the living room, standing before the fireplace, talking to each other. They had turned off most of the lights, and there was only the soft glow from some lamps and the flickering fireplace. It looked warm in the room, cozy.

He saw her come to the window, right across the street from where he was standing, and gaze out into the night. She looked so young and nice that for a moment he was sorry he was going to kill her. Then she stretched out her hand and pulled a curtain across the window, and it was as though she had reached across the street and slapped him in the face. His moment of weakness passed. She deserved to be killed and he would feel no remorse when he had killed her.

He moved to the back of the boathouse and began walking slowly along the water, disappearing in a shroud of fog.

CHAPTER TWO

O<small>N THE TENTH OF</small> No-
vember, having driven down from Boston to catch the
midmorning ferry, the first thing Mr. Timothy O'Hara did
in Edgartown was find the office of the *Vineyard Gazette*.
He asked the young woman behind the desk near the front
door of the old Colonial house who had covered the
Barrow murder trial for the paper.

"Ken Lambert," the woman said.

"Is Mr. Lambert in?"

"No, he's playing tennis."

"Tennis? In this weather? Oh, indoors, I guess."

"No, outdoors. He's a tennis nut. He's been known to
shovel snow to play."

"Do you know where he's playing?"

"At the yacht club courts," she said, and she told him
how to get there. Mr. O'Hara thanked her for the information.

He had no trouble finding Pease's Point Way. He
turned right onto it and a minute or two later was parking his car in the lot before the clubhouse. There were,
not to O'Hara's surprise, only two players on the chilly

11

courts. One of them was a stalwart young woman, so O'Hara deduced that her opponent was Ken Lambert.

The two of them were good players, well matched; O'Hara was not bored during the thirty-five minutes it took them to finish their final set. He watched them, though, wistfully. In his day he had been an athlete. High school football and baseball, then bowling, until his legs gave out. Now in his middle sixties he couldn't walk a hundred yards before cramps in his calves hobbled him.

The woman rode victoriously off on a bicycle. O'Hara approached her victim as he was opening his car door and introduced himself.

"Hi." Ken Lambert was a pleasant fellow somewhere in his late thirties and evidently a good loser. "Something I can do for you?"

"Yes, there is, thanks. You covered the Barrow murder case for the *Gazette?*"

"Right."

"I'm researching what I hope will be a magazine article on the trial."

"Why? It's been more than three years since the murder. So what's the angle on a story at this late date? Why drag it all up again?"

"Well, now Nancy Barrow is married to David Webster, of the Boston Back Bay Websters. And I understand she's back on the Vineyard with him."

"Yes, that's right."

"There are some people who think that she should not have been acquitted, that a Boston Webster has married a murderess. That seems an angle to me. Was she guilty or not? What do you think?"

"Well, I wouldn't want to be quoted. I'm an old friend of the Ryans, Nancy's parents. In fact Nancy's father helped me through Amherst. I've known them ever

12

since they bought the house on Cooke Street, and Nancy wasn't more than four or five then."

"They still here?" O'Hara asked. "Her parents?"

"No, they're both dead. A boating accident off Gay Head several years ago. It would have been awful rough on Mr. and Mrs. Ryan, their daughter's murder trial."

"You don't want me to quote you," O'Hara said, "because I gather you thought she was guilty. You didn't—look, my legs . . . mind if I sit down? I'm feeling my age. Prematurely, I contend, but my legs don't agree."

Lambert invited him to take a seat in his car. They climbed into it and the host extended his hospitality. "I happen to have a pint of rum in the glove compartment," he said. "Don't know how it got there, this time of the morning. Care for a swig?"

"A swig of rum," O'Hara said. "Never turn down an offer like that, any time of the morning."

They each had a swig of rum, then on second thought, a second swig, and they smiled at each other. Then, seriously, Lambert said, "Yes, I'm afraid I do."

"Do what? Oh, yes," O'Hara said. "I asked a question and that's your answer. You think she was guilty."

"That's right, damn it," Lambert said. "She shot him all right. And she tried to make it look as though it had been a robbery, as if a burglar had killed him. And I must say she got away with it at first. No weapon was found, which indicated the intruder had taken it with him. A window on the first floor was open. The place had been ransacked and the jewelry she'd inherited from her mother was missing. Pretty clever. An open-and-shut case, the cops thought—but they only thought that for about twenty-four hours."

"What made them think different?"

"Nancy made two big mistakes. The gun, which had

13

belonged to her father, for God's sake, was found the next morning in a flower box next to the side door. And there were two witnesses who saw her scrabbling in that flower box at about the time of the murder. Obviously, she was burying the gun."

"She must have panicked," O'Hara said, "letting two people see her. Did she try to deny it?"

"Oh, no, she admitted she'd been at the flower box. But she said that when she came home the door had been locked, and she was looking for an extra key that she kept hidden there."

"Nobody was buying that story, I guess."

"Nobody. And after that the missing jewelry was found in the house. Hidden cleverly, but not cleverly enough. Nancy denied everything, of course, but the defense knew they were beaten from the start. They didn't even pretend there was a burglar." Lambert glanced at the clock on his dashboard. "Good Lord, I've got to get moving. If there's anything more I can tell you . . . but, sorry, not right now."

"Could I see the files on the case—get the names of the witnesses, the people involved?"

"Of course. Just go to the office and ask for them."

"Thanks for your help," O'Hara said. "And you play good tennis and serve good rum."

On his second day on the island O'Hara woke up, looked out the window of his room at the Daggett House and found that the neighboring island of Chappaquiddick had disappeared in the denseness of the morning fog. It was seven twenty by his watch. He shaved and showered quickly, ate a hearty breakfast, and at exactly eight o'clock he was climbing the steps to the top deck of the town dock. By that time the fog had lifted slightly, but it still hung in whorls over the dock. He watched the small three-car ferry come from Chappaquiddick, its only passengers a few children in a bright yellow school bus.

To rest his legs, wearied by the climb, he sat on one of the dock's long benches and turned to look back at the town. In a few minutes he saw her coming toward the pier. He recognized her from the pictures he had seen in the *Vineyard Gazette* the afternoon before. She was walking quickly—striding—and when she reached the bottom of the steps he could see that her face was flushed with anger.

She climbed to the top deck, saw that he was alone there, and came directly to him.

"Mr. O'Hara," she said, "I'm Nancy Webster."

"Of course," he said. "And you're upset. Why?"

"It happened again, just now on Main Street. Two women I've known since I was a child, two of my mother's best friends, staring at me from across the street, whispering about me behind their hands. I couldn't hear what they were saying, but I could feel it. Nancy Ryan, murderer, husband-killer, returning to the scene of her crime. Mr. O'Hara, I hope you're going to put a stop to that."

"That's what I'm here for, Mrs. Webster."

"I'm sorry I missed you at the agency the other day."

"Agency? What agency?" O'Hara asked in mock confusion. "Are you mistaking me for a detective maybe? No, I'm a writing fellow, Mrs. Webster, come to the Vineyard to do some research."

She grinned. "How is that going? Your disguise, I mean. Or cover, I guess the word is."

"Very well, so far," O'Hara said. "Yesterday I convinced a chap—a writer himself, a reporter—that I was doing a magazine piece."

15

"Nice going," Nancy said. "You do understand why I don't want anyone to know who you are or what you're doing."

"Of course."

"I haven't told anyone, not even my husband."

"But you intend to tell him?"

"Oh, yes. He's been in New York, seeing his publisher. I'll tell him tomorrow night when he gets home. I'm sure he'll understand why I have to do this."

"May I ask why you've waited so long?"

"Well, I never thought I'd ever want to come back to the Vineyard, so it didn't matter to me what people thought. But after Dave and I were married . . . well, he's spent almost every summer of his life here and he loves it. And now that he's writing, we can live here all year round."

O'Hara nodded. "Great little island you've got here. I can understand his wanting to—"

"Oh, no, it was my idea! All mine." Nancy said. "I told Dave I wanted to try it. I knew it wouldn't be easy, there would be people who believed I was guilty. But my friends, the people I've known all my life—I was sure they knew I was innocent. I was counting on them."

"I gather you were disappointed."

"They're so kind, Mr. O'Hara," she said bitterly, "and oh, so very tactful. They act as though it had never happened—no murder, no trial, nothing. But they think I'm guilty! They have forgiven me, they don't even blame me, but they think I'm guilty! In less than a week I saw that it wasn't working . . . and it never will unless I'm proven innocent. And you, Mr. O'Hara, are the boy who's going to do just that, right?"

"I'll do my damned best."

"You must have questions to ask me. . . ."

16

"Not quite yet. Suppose you call me at the Daggett House tomorrow morning, and we'll arrange to get together somewhere."

"Right," Nancy said. "Nice meeting you, Mr. O'Hara. Very, very nice. I feel better already. So long for now."

"So long, Mrs. Webster."

He watched her disappear down the dock steps. Then he turned to look over the water. This was going to be one hell of a job. He knew that Andrews, his boss, wouldn't have touched this case himself with a ten-foot pole, and he knew why it had been handed to him. And that hurt. By God it did.

On his last several jobs he hadn't done well—two of them he had messed up badly. And then his legs, his goddamn aching legs. Andrews thought of him as an old, used-up man. He wanted to unload him. He had given him a case that was impossible to solve favorably to the client, one that would mean another failure for O'Hara. And another failure could certainly justify his being fired.

On the other hand, if he could bring it off, turn an impossible assignment into a success and prove the girl not guilty—hope surged momentarily in O'Hara, then dropped like a wounded sparrow. It looked worse than impossible. But, by God, he'd give it a try. He would, as he had told the young lady, do his damned best.

The man was sitting on the stairs leading to the upper deck when he heard her footsteps on the floor above him. Swiftly, without getting to his feet, he hitched down the steps, and walked to the other side of the dock. It didn't matter. She didn't look right or left—just hurried up to Water Street and turned south onto it.

In a few minutes the man she had been talking to

followed her down, but slowly, very slowly. He got in a car that was parked beside the ferry slip and drove away. It was the same man he had seen in town yesterday, old and sort of fat, talking to Ken Lambert by the tennis courts.

So the old guy was a detective, trying to prove that Nancy Ryan hadn't killed her husband. Maybe he could do that—yeah, maybe in a million years. The trouble was the old guy didn't have a million years. In a couple of days it would be all over, and who would care if she was guilty or not once she was dead?

He had learned the one thing he needed to know: David Webster was coming back to the island tomorrow. That was all he had to know to put his plan into effect. and then Nancy Ryan would have to pay for her wickedness—for the bad thing she had done and the lies she had told, for the deceit.

One thing he had to remember; in the next days he must go on the way he always did, he must go about his business as if nothing was happening. That way nothing could go wrong; he would be all right.

Putting his hands in his pockets, he walked leisurely off the dock and up the street. It was time now to go about his business.

CHAPTER THREE

*B*Y ONE O'CLOCK the early fog had been burned off by an aggressive wintry sun, and the day was bright and cold and windless. O'Hara had spent most of the morning familiarizing himself with the village, driving up and down the streets of Edgartown. He had twice passed the lofty white house on Water Street where Nancy Webster was now living, and had stopped before the one on Cooke Street where she had lived during the summer as a child, and where three years ago her husband was murdered. A family from Montreal had bought it, he had been told, and it was empty now, closed for the winter. He got out of his car and stood on the sidewalk, looking at the house.

It was a trim Colonial, its shingles weathered to a silver sheen, faded blue shutters at the windows, flower boxes of the same blue beneath them. He looked thoughtfully at the flower box by the side door, the one in which the murder weapon had been found. He walked slowly around the house, picking out the window on the ground floor that had been found open on the night of the murder, through which the killer was supposed to have fled. He shook his head. The house on

Cooke Street could certainly tell him nothing. he got back in his car.

He wanted to find a man named Andy Fisher who worked as a gardener in the summer and as a caretaker for the closed houses of summer residents the rest of the year. His name had been mentioned in the *Gazette* file in connection with the Barrow murder case.

A kid at a local gas station had told him that Andy would probably be working today at the Morton place on School Street. He would recognize the house, the kid said, because Andy's blue Chevrolet pickup truck would be parked outside. O'Hara spotted the truck in the middle of the block; he knew it was the right one because on both doors, stencilled in bright red, were the letters A N D Y. He spotted Andy himself just as he finished repairing a step on the Morton front porch. O'Hara parked and watched Andy put his carpenter's tools in the back of his truck, and take his gardener's tools out of it. Then, with a pair of clippers in hand, he knelt to trim some bronze chrysanthemums that were fading into winter hibernation on either side of the steps.

O'Hara saw that Andy was about forty, a small but sturdy man, no more than five foot, five, with a slight, almost imperceptible limp. He was smiling as he worked. O'Hara couldn't see anything that he should be especially happy about, except possibly having a job well done on the porch steps. But as he trimmed the mums the smile changed to a frown of frozen concentration. He was beheading the flowers, some still brightly alive, but he was not executing them. He was operating on them like some skilled surgeon. It was instantly apparent to O'Hara that he was a dedicated gardener.

"You're Andy Fisher, aren't you?" O'Hara asked.

"That's right." The dedicated gardener glanced up at

O'Hara, then went back to his trimming. "Don't think I know you, though, do I?"

O'Hara explained, as he had to Ken Lambert, why he was in Edgartown, what he was doing. Researching the Barrow murder case for a magazine article he was writing.

"I don't read much," Andy said, "except for stuff about gardening. I read the *Gazette*, though—every issue." He had finished with the flowers; he stood up, pocketing the clippers. "How you doing to write this article? You going to write that she was guilty or not guilty?"

"I'm trying to find out the truth. And that's what I'll write. I've been talking to people here, Andy, and reading the files in the newspaper office. You claimed you saw someone at the Barrow house that night."

"The Ryan house," Andy corrected. "We still call it the Ryan house. Yes, I saw someone."

"Tell me about it."

"Well, I was over on Cooke Street that night—"

"Why, Andy? What were you doing?"

"I got to worrying about the furnace in the Fitzsimmons house. We had snow that afternoon, a light snow, but the temperature was falling. I was afraid of a bad freeze. That furnace was balky, if it conked out the pipes could freeze. My first chance, about nine that night, I went over and checked. It was okay. Coming back I saw the man in the Ryan's back yard."

"The paper said you didn't recognize him—you couldn't describe him."

"He was too far away. I could just see it was a man, that's all."

"Was there anyone else around who might have seen him?"

Andy shook his head. "I passed old Mr. Danbury on

21

Cooke Street, but he was coming the other way. No, I don't think he could have seen him."

"It was winter, Andy, and dark by nine o'clock. Mightn't you have been wrong?"

"No, I wasn't wrong. I saw a man in the back yard."

"But the police found no footprints under the open window. If it had been snowing, there would have been prints."

"Maybe he did something to erase them," Andy said. "Like I sometimes erase my footprints when I'm gardening. To neaten up."

"You didn't testify at the trial, did you? About the man you saw."

"No. I said I would, but they wouldn't let me."

"Why not?"

"They didn't think anyone would believe me," Andy said, resentment sounding in his voice. "They didn't believe me themselves. Even her own lawyers thought she was guilty."

"And you didn't think so?"

"No. I've known her nearly all her life, and I know she couldn't kill anybody. Look, why do you want to write about it, anyhow? It's all over and I don't want to talk about it any more."

Andy turned on his heel and strode down the walk to the street. Walking rapidly his limp was accentuated, strongly pronounced; an awkward lurching gait. O'Hara watched him climb into his Chevy pickup and drive away. A minute later O'Hara got carefully into his car. His legs were hurting.

That evening Ken Lambert covered a town meeting at which some rezoning was debated. There was quite a lot of name-calling, but no violence. Still, it made a good

22

story, and he hurried from the meeting to his office to write it. He became absorbed in his writing and did two rewrites. It was after ten when he got home.

Claire was still downstairs, waiting for him, reading. He considered her the most attractive and charming girl ever to graduate from Smith, and he thanked heaven once a day for seeing to it that he had got to Amherst, and for arranging the blind date that brought them together. They had been married fifteen years.

"The meeting interesting?" she asked. "Any blood shed?"

"No, but there were some fine harsh words exchanged."

"So you could write a good story."

"I could and I did. I'm so pleased with myself I'm going to have a very strong nightcap. Join me?"

"No, thanks," Claire said, but she followed him into the kitchen. She got a glass for him and went to the refrigerator for ice, while he got his bottle of Scotch.

"Amy asleep?"

"Probably not quite. She just went up. For Christmas she wants her own telephone in her own room and—"

"Hey!" Ken said. "How about this?"

Claire turned to him. He was holding the bottle up for her to see.

"What about it?"

"It's practically empty. There were at least a couple of shots left last time I looked."

"Are you sure?" Claire asked.

"Positive. And you don't drink Scotch . . ."

"Oh, damn!" Clair said. "I wanted to surprise you."

"Surprise me how? With an empty Scotch bottle? Ha-ha. Pardon my hollow laughter, but did you pour it down the drain to surprise me? If you did, it worked."

"No, you're always asking me to have a drink or two

with you. Or three, on weekends. So I've been practicing. I've been taking nips now and then. You know Scotch is an acquired taste, don't you? Well, I've been acquiring it. Nothing is too much for the man I love."

Now Ken's laugh was genuine. "So we could drink together this weekend you acquired a taste so fast that there isn't any Scotch left for the weekend."

"I was going to buy some in the morning."

"Better buy it by the barrel."

"You're embarrassing me, Ken."

"I'm kidding you, Claire. Look, I was counting on that nightcap. When I parked the car I noticed that the Bells were watching hockey and having beer. Mind if I bum a drink of Scotch from them?"

"And watch a little hockey? Not at all, go ahead. Be their guest."

When the door closed behind him, she went to a window and watched him being greeted by the Bells, their neighbors, and welcomed into the house. Claire stood at the window for a few minutes, looking out into the night. Then she took a deep breath and went upstairs. The door to Amy's room was closed. She opened it, switched on the light. Amy sat up in bed, startled. She was twelve, small for her age, with yellow hair in tidy pigtails and wide, innocent brown eyes.

"I want to talk to you, Amy," Claire said.

"Oh-oh," Amy said. "I know that look, Mother! You're not going to talk, you're going to scold. What did I do this time?"

"I'm doing my best," her mother said, "not to scold."

"Great! I'll help you. Let's skip the whole thing. Daddy home yet?"

"Yes, Daddy's been home. He wanted a nightcap. There wasn't enough Scotch left for him to have one."

"Oh," Amy said.

24

"You drank it, didn't you?" Amy didn't answer. "Don't bother to deny it, Amy. I know you did."

"Does Daddy know? Did you tell him?"

"No, I didn't. I know how angry he would have been. I told him I drank it."

"Thanks, Mom. You're a pal!"

"I shouldn't have been a pal," her mother said. "Amy, if this ever happens again I'm going to tell your father. Because we'll have to keep the liquor locked up."

"Oh, Mom, you're making such a big deal out of this! It's only the second time it's happened!"

"And you promised me the first time it would never happen again."

"Look, just because I took a couple of sips—"

"More than just a couple of sips."

"Just a little more. And I had some help."

"Who?"

"Mom, don't make me tell you . . . oh, damn, you don't believe me, do you? Okay, it was Betty Lou."

"Little Betty Lou Weaver?"

"She's as old as I am! Are you going to tell her mother?"

"No, not this time. But if it ever happens again I'm going to tell your Father and Betty Lou's mother."

Amy laughed. "That's blackmail, sort of."

Her mother smiled, but grimly. "Yes, sort of, but I mean it. Good night now."

"Good night . . . hey, Mom!"

"What?"

"I don't really like Scotch."

"Glad to hear it, dear."

"Couldn't you get Daddy to switch to gin?"

"You brat," her mother said, stifling a smile.

"Mom, I'll try to get better grades, too."

"That's my girl."

CHAPTER FOUR

CARL DANZIG, the Chief of Police, was a native of the island, and O'Hara could see that he would have had it no other way; in just the few minutes he had been in Danzig's office, O'Hara could feel the Chief's pride in his job, his team. He was a middle-aged man, affable and friendly; but also tough.

"No," he was telling O'Hara, "there wasn't any man in the Ryans' back yard that night. Andy Fisher made that up."

"Why?" O'Hara asked. "Why would he do that?"

"He was trying to help Nancy."

"Of course," O'Hara said. "Bad question. I meant, why would he try to help her? What's the connection there? It certainly isn't an obvious one—wait, let me guess. Andy is a gardener. He was Nancy's parents' gardener, right?"

"Right on the nose," the Chief said. "The Ryans' gardener and caretaker, but he and Nancy had a special relationship. You noticed Andy's leg—his limp?"

"Yes. It's very slight, except when he's in a hurry. Polio before Dr. Salk?"

"No. One afternoon when Andy was clipping the

Ryans' hedges, Nancy—she was just a little kid then—ran out into the street in front of a truck. Andy dove after her, knocked her out of the way, but he got hit. Did that to his leg."

"So Andy maybe saved her life."

"Well, there was no way to prove that," the Chief said, "but the Ryans were grateful all right. And Andy and little Nancy became pals, buddies. I remember it. Cute. The little girl following the gardener all over town. So you see, there is a special connection."

"And," O'Hara said, "it's not surprising he would try to help her when she was up on a murder charge. Well, that takes care of that point. Let's see . . . next question. Which one of your men answered the call the night of the murder? He still around?"

"Yes," the Chief said. "Al Potter."

"That's right, Mr. O'Hara," Al Potter said. "I was cruising out on Planting Field Way when my radio told me to go to the Ryan house on Cooke Street."

"If I've got your streets lined up right," O'Hara said, "you must have gotten there in just a few minutes."

"I didn't waste any time," Potter said.

"Do you remember what time it was when you got there?"

Potter nodded. "Mrs. Barrow called the station at nine thirty-five. So say it was about nine forty when I got to the house."

"Did you know what to expect? That Barrow had been killed?"

"Yeah, I knew that."

"How was Mrs. Barrow? Was she hysterical, or under control, or what?"

"Well, she seemed to be in shock. She met me at the

door and led me back to the den where the body was. She said that she had walked in and found him just like that. She didn't think she had touched anything."

"She called the police right away?"

"I asked her that and she said she didn't know. She told me she'd stood there for a while just staring at her husband's body, not able to believe it. It might have been a minute or two, or maybe five or six. She didn't know."

"Did you believe her?"

"Yes, it can happen like that. People in an accident or caught up in violence; some of them go into shock, lose all sense of time. I had no reason not to believe her."

"What did you do then?"

"Well, I looked around to see if there was a weapon, and there wasn't. I noticed the open window in the dining room; and going through the house I saw open drawers, signs of ransacking. I asked Mrs. Barrow if she felt up to looking to see if anything was missing and she said she would try. After a few minutes she told me her jewelry was gone. By that time Dr. Rankin had arrived. He'd had to come from the hospital at Oak Bluffs."

"He set the time of the death?"

"The best he could do was to say that Barrow had been dead for anywhere from half an hour to fifty minutes. That meant the murder occurred somewhere between ten past nine and nine thirty."

"And of course Mrs. Barrow didn't have an alibi for those twenty minutes."

"No."

"What do you think about it, Officer? Off the record, of course. I suppose like most people here you'd known Nancy Ryan since she was a kid."

"No, I'm not an Islander, I transferred here from the force at Buzzard's Bay a little more than three years ago.

I knew who she was, of course, but not to speak to."

"Did you think she was guilty?"

Al Potter shrugged. On the record or off, he was not going to commit himself. "The jury acquitted her," was all he had to say.

It was two o'clock, and he was standing near the corner of Green Street when he saw her drive past in the car that was small and low and painted fire engine red. She was going fast, and in a minute the car had vanished; but it was all right. It didn't matter.

After he had heard her tell the detective fellow that David would be coming back tonight, he had telephoned the airport and asked about planes from New York City. David would have had to take the shuttle to Boston, and get a plane to the Vineyard from there. He wouldn't arrive on the Vineyard until seven. So there was time, there was plenty of time, for what he had to do.

He had it all worked out, carefully and perfectly, and nothing was going wrong. It was going to happen soon now, and when it did, what a fuss there would be! Like when her first husband had been murdered. Police from the mainland would come swarming to the island, and newspaper people and television people would come from everywhere. There would be lots of lights and cameras all over town, and they would be interviewing everybody on the Vineyard and asking them what they knew and where they had been and what they had seen.

Everybody except him. They wouldn't be asking him anything, because nobody would connect him with what had happened. He would just go about his business, knowing that what he had done was a good thing, the right thing; that Nancy Ryan had deserved it.

And down inside he would be laughing at them all.

Just outside the village Nancy swung onto the narrow road that led to Clam Bay. The little settlement there was completely deserted, the dozen or so houses closed and shuttered for the winter. She parked her car on the hard, packed sand at the edge of the beach.

It was one of those bright and sparkling days that sometimes comes to the Vineyard in November, the sky and sea the same shade of blue, with small, playful waves breaking on the rocks near the shore and sending up a shower of crystal spray. There were no footprints marring the smooth clean sand, nothing but clusters of broken shells, and here and there a clump of winter-blackened beach plums or silver-gray bayberries. It was the kind of summerlike fall day she remembered from her childhood, when her family had brought her to the island for Thanksgiving.

She had been coming to this place every day for the past week, ever since Dave had been away, walking for miles up and down the beach. Here she had felt hopeful and happy, and she had spent hours envisioning the charmed life she and Dave would lead on the island. But not today. She had spent most of the morning in the winter seclusion of the bird refuge at Sherriff's Meadow with the detective Timothy O'Hara, answering his probing questions, and now, the past was too much with her.

O'Hara had had her go back to the beginning when, as an only child, she lived with her parents in a sprawling old apartment near Gramercy Park in New York, with summers spent in the house here on Cooke Street. At fifteen she had gone off to the boarding school of her choice, with more jolly summers at the Vineyard. At eighteen she had started college at Ann Arbor, and that year had been the last of carefree young life for her; her mother and father, spending a spring weekend on the island, had been drowned when their boat caught fire and sank off Gay Head.

O'Hara had wanted to know about Jim Barrow. Nancy had met him when he was a senior at Ann Arbor, toward the end of her sophomore year. He had been unlike any of the boys she had known before; rough and tough and macho, dazzling his way through college on a football scholarship. On their first date she had thought him the handsomest and most exciting man on earth. She had gone to bed with him on their second date and by that time she was committed; she was head over heels in love.

They had been married on the day he graduated. There had been no reason to wait; she had only a few distant and scattered relatives, and Jim, having finished almost at the top of his class, had job offers from all over the country. After a short wedding trip, he had immediately gone to work for the Richards Chemical Company in Chicago.

She had told the detective about their first year there; and how the following June they had come to the island to live in her family's house on Cooke Street, which had been left to her, and Jim had opened a sporting goods shop on Main Street. Five months later he had been murdered.

The trial had been a nightmare, with her resolutely protesting her innocence and every witness disproving her. It was almost over when her lawyer had called up a surprise witness, a witness who was a shocking surprise to Nancy. She had turned her head away in anger and humiliation.

The witness said her name was Gloria Seidman, and she lived at 1350 Lake Shore Drive in Chicago. She was employed in the personnel department of the Richards

31

Chemical Company, also in Chicago. She had known Jim Barrow the year that he had been employed by the same company, and she and Nancy Barrow had become good friends.

"Will you tell the jury," Nancy's lawyer had asked Gloria Seidman, "what happened on the night of May tenth that year?"

"Jim had said he was going to work late at the office that night," Gloria said, "and Nancy and I planned to go to a movie. I drove to their apartment to pick her up. I rang the bell, but no one answered. The television was turned on, quite loud, and I thought perhaps she hadn't heard me ringing. I tried the door and it was open, so I went in and I . . . ." The witness hesitated, then stopped.

"Please go on, Miss Seidman. You went into the apartment."

"Yes. Nancy was lying on a couch in the living room. Her nose was bleeding, and her lip and her eye swollen. Her clothes were torn and one breast was badly beaten. I ran into the bedroom where the phone was to call a doctor and the police. Jim Barrow was sitting there, very quietly, as though he were dazed. There was blood on his hands."

"Did you phone a doctor, Miss Seidman? Or the police?"

"No, I did not."

"Why not?"

"Because Nancy wouldn't let me. She told me not to do anything. She said she could take care of herself, it wasn't the first time it had happened. She said she would be all right. And she asked me to go."

"So you never reported this?"

"Not to the police, no. I reported it the next day in the office and Jim Barrow was discharged."

After Gloria Seidman had left the stand a Chicago

physician testified that three months earlier, in February of that year, he had treated Nancy Barrow for injuries that she claimed she had sustained in a fall down a flight of stairs, but that he was certain had been the result of a severe beating.

Dr. Jared Rankin, of Edgartown, was then called to the stand. He said that in the five months between June, when Nancy and Jim Barrow had moved into the house on Cooke Street, and November, when the murder had occurred, Nancy had come to his office twice to be treated for lacerations and bruises. Both times she had told him she had fallen, and both times he was convinced that she had been beaten.

The trial had ended the next day, and that afternoon the jury had brought in its verdict. Nancy Barrow had been found not guilty.

CHAPTER FIVE

*A*MY LAMBERT and her very best friend, Betty Lou Weaver, were in the same American history class. This afternoon, as she did every school day when the dismissal bell rang, Betty Lou waited in the corridor for Amy so they could walk together to their last classes; Betty Lou to math, Amy to English.

"Wow!" Amy said.

"Wow what?" Betty Lou asked, immediately intrigued and concerned by the drama in her friend's voice.

"Last night!"

"What happened last night? Amy, tell me!"

"My mother! No, first my father! He noticed there was some Scotch missing out of his bottle."

"Oh, no!"

"Oh, yes!"

"But we didn't drink much—just a couple of sips each."

"It was enough for my father to notice. And he told my mother. and guess what?" Amy asked proudly. "I bet you can't guess what?"

"No, I can't," Betty Lou said. "Not in a million years. What?"

"My mother took the blame."

"Boy, oh, boy! What a mother!"

"But she told me if I ever did it again she would tell my father on me." The two girls stopped in front of Betty Lou's classroom. "So we can't sneak any more of my father's Scotch. If only your family weren't anti-booze!"

"I know. It's so old-fashioned."

"Well," Amy said, "there's only one way out. We'll just have to take another bike ride some night soon and stock up."

Unfriendly clouds had started blocking out the sun's warmth, and the beach was no longer a pleasant place to be. It was suddenly, in fact, cold and damp and uncomfortable. Nancy turned and hurried back toward the cluster of houses that overlooked Clam Bay. She got in her car and turned on the ignition, but nothing happened. She tried it again. And again. Nothing. She swore a bit. That didn't help. She knew she wasn't out of gas; she had filled the tank just yesterday. Something else was wrong, something beyond her knowledge of car engines. Her precious little car, a wedding present from David, until now so trusty and adorable, had failed her. But as she got out and walked helplessly around it, it looked so ashamed of itself that she forgave it. She patted it consolingly on its hood.

After all it was only about a mile's hike to the nearest garage, less than that to a telephone in the nearest occupied house. Then she thought of David. It didn't seem possible that the car could be repaired in time for her to meet him at the airport. But she could rent a car at the garage, or she could walk a mile farther to their house and borrow Mrs. MacWilliam's car. Mrs. Mac had gone with a friend to spend the day on the Cape, but the key to her car was hanging in the kitchen by the sink. If there wasn't time for that she could call the airport, have David paged, and tell him to take a cab. She had to laugh at herself. Never had a problem had so many obvious solutions. But whatever the solution, she would soon be seeing David. And from now on, she decided, whenever he went off-island, even for a day, she was going with him.

"Until now," she told herself, "maybe you haven't realized how much, how absolutely head over positively heels you are in love with him."

David, who through her teens had been her summertime comrade, had come back into her life when she had most needed someone, right after Jim Barrow's murder. He had been there when she was awaiting trial, and during it, and in the dreary years that followed. And somewhere along the way they had discovered, to their mutual surprise and pleasure, that they were in love.

She started hiking, thinking enthusiastically about how much she loved David . . . let's see, more than Heloise loved Abelard, more than Antony and Caesar put together loved Cleopatra . . . Again she had to laugh at herself. Being in love made her ever so foolish, but didn't it do that to everyone? Juliet, for instance? Listening to that old Friar Lawrence. How did it go? . . . "Take thou this vial, being then in bed, and presently through thy veins shall run . . . a deep and pleasant sleep"? Result: disaster. And then she saw a blue pickup truck start out of the driveway of one of the closed Clam Bay houses. It was Andy Fisher's truck, and it was Andy driving it, and she was pleased as Punch himself to see him.

36

"Andy! Hey, Andy!"

He saw her and drove his truck down to the edge of the sand, jumped out, and ran, with his clumsy, shuffling gait, to meet her. "Nancy! I heard you were back."

She took his outstretched hand in both of hers. "Yeah. I've been hoping I'd run into you soon. How are you, anyway, Andy?"

"I'm okay, Nancy. Same as ever."

"You look great, Andy. Better than ever."

"You too, Nancy. Say, what's the matter? Having trouble with your car?"

"Not really. It just won't start, that's all."

"Well, you know me, I'm not much of a mechanic, but I'll be glad to take a look."

They walked over to the ailing car and Andy lifted the hood. He stared down at the intricate maze of machinery and shook his head.

"These foreign cars are too much for me. Don't even know where to look. Sure you aren't out of gas?"

"I'm almost full."

"Well, best I can do for you is give you a lift to the garage. You still go to Ollie's"

"Yes."

They started back to the pickup.

"I heard you'd come back here to live. All year round."

"That's right, Andy."

"You and your folks, you sure loved this old island." He opened the truck door for her. "It's good to have you back."

"Thanks, Andy, and thanks for the lift."

"Sure, glad to do it." He climbed in behind the wheel. "What are you doing out here at Clam Bay? Taking care of somebody's house?"

"The Kenyon place. You remember them, Nancy,

they own the big hotel in town."

"Oh, sure. Remember when you helped me put the sand shark in the hotel swimming pool?"

He nodded. "You were ten years old. Not much bigger than that fish."

"And remember how those three ladies screamed when they saw it?"

"Dumbbells," Andy said. He reached between his feet down to the floor of the truck. "Everybody knows sand sharks won't hurt you."

"Yeah, but they are kind of scary looking—"

Andy swiveled suddenly toward her, and with his right arm he pinioned her against the seat. She looked at him in astonishment. "Andy, hey—" she said. "What the hell—"

With his left hand he slapped the sponge, which was drenched with chloroform, across her nose and mouth. She struggled furiously, but she was no match for Andy Fisher. Then her struggling ceased, and she was unconscious.

Timothy O'Hara got in his car and drove toward School Street, where in five minutes he had an appointment with Mrs. Mickey Jamison, long-time friend of Nancy Webster. He had phoned her in the morning at the Island Realty Company where she was employed. She had pleaded a work-filled day at her office, and invited him to call on her at home at eight that evening.

He parked in front of the Jamison house. It was a prefab Cape Cod cottage, with a white picket fence enclosing a neat, small lawn. The knocker on the door was made of lead, and shaped like a whale. When he rapped it a faraway voice shouted for him to come in. He stepped into an empty living room and called a hello.

"Mr. O'Hara?"

He admitted he was.

"I'm in the kitchen."

He found the kitchen. Mickey Jamison, a buxom, robust young woman in her middle twenties, was at the sink. The sink was filled with water and some unattractive, stringy black vegetable matter. She was slushing her hands in it.

"Oh-oh!" O'Hara said. "Sink stopped up?"

She laughed heartily. "Can't wait to tell my hubby that! No, Mr. O'Hara, I'm sort of an artist. See?"

She jerked her head toward the kitchen table. O'Hara saw several dozen folded cards standing like tiny tents. They were decorated with wet weed arranged in some surprisingly pretty floral designs.

"Place cards," Mickey explained. "Sea moss place cards." She dipped a clean card into the water beneath the weeds and steered some moss onto it with a toothpick, then spread the moss, separating its strands into what this time might be a Christmas tree. "There, that's a good one! Do you mind if I finish? I got the moss yesterday, and if I don't use it tonight it'll spoil."

"No, you go right ahead. Very interesting."

"And you go right ahead, Mr. O'Hara. Ask me your questions. I didn't realize it was time for you to come. I never know what time it is. What time is it?"

"Ten past eight. Ten minutes past eight p.m. to be exact."

"Oh, I know that much," Mickey said with a giggle. "It's after dark. I didn't graduate from high school for nothing! Met Warren there. Sorry he isn't home. Volunteer fireman's meeting."

"Well, you know I want to talk about Nancy Webster. And I heard you were old friends."

"Yes, we are, but until she married Jim Barrow and came here to live year round, we were only part-time friends.

Nancy and her family were summer people, and I'm an Islander. So for about fifteen years I was only Nancy's friend for . . . let's see, fifteen times three months is forty-five months. Right?"

"Right," O'Hara said. "You really didn't waste your time in high school."

Mickey laughed. "There, that's enough place cards to seat a small army. Let's go into the living room, okay?"

"Okay."

He followed her into the front room. "There on the wall over the television set," she said. "That's my masterpiece."

"That," O'Hara said admiringly, "is the most irate seaweed ostrich I've ever seen."

"Thanks, but not seaweed. Sea moss. So, yes, Nancy and I were good friends. Summers, I used to spend a lot of time at the Ryan house. Her mother and father were terrific people. When they got killed in the boat accident . . . God, the rotten things that have happened to Nancy. Her life with Jim Barrow. . .those beatings. . ."
She stopped, shaking her head at the thought.

"Did you know about them?"

"Not until it came out at the trial. No one did. Afterward, when she'd been acquitted and I went to see her in New York, she told me a little about it—about why Jim did what he did, why she stayed with him. All that."

"Did he have a drinking problem?"

She nodded. "Apparently the big job in Chicago was too much for him. The pressures were too great, and he started drinking. And when he drank, he mistreated her. And she stayed with him for the same reasons other battered wives stay with their husbands, I guess. Guilt, helplessness . . . and pride. Nancy's a very proud person. And of course Jim was always sorry about what he'd done afterward. He always swore it wouldn't happen again."

"And she wanted to believe that."

"Sure. And when they finally found out about it in Chicago and fired Jim, then she really did think it would stop. They used Nancy's inheritance to buy the sporting goods store here, and they moved into the Ryan house. It was going to be a new life for them. No problems. No drinking. Well, you know it didn't work out that way. Jim began drinking again—he started beating Nancy again. And it probably would have gone on forever if..."

"If he hadn't been murdered," O'Hara finished.

"Yes, I'm afraid so."

"That's what I want to talk to you about, Mrs. Jamison. You saw Nancy the night of the murder."

"Yes."

"Tell me about it."

"I was on my way home," Mickey said. "As I was driving past Nancy's house I saw her at the side door. She was bending over the flower box there."

"And she claims she was getting a door key she kept hidden there, not burying a gun. What did you think she was doing?"

Mickey shook her head. "My headlights picked her up for just an instant. I saw her bending over the flower box, period. I couldn't tell what she was doing."

"Tell me—what time was it when you passed the house?" O'Hara said.

"The police kept asking me that. Like I told you, I never know what time it is. The best I could tell them was that it was sometime between nine o'clock and nine thirty. But Ethel Winston says—have you talked to her?"

"Not yet," O'Hara said. "She's off-island someplace today."

"Well, Ethel says when she saw Nancy at the flower box it was exactly nine twenty, so I suppose that's when it was."

"And," O'Hara said, "she testified that Nancy was at the flower box for at least three minutes. Which was long enough for her to bury a gun."

"I know," Mickey said unhappily. "Like I said, I only saw her for a second. She could have been getting a key *or* burying a gun, to be absolutely honest about it. If only I had stopped that night and talked to Nancy—that might have changed everything."

"You seem pretty sure," O'Hara said, "that you would have found her looking for her key."

"Oh, Mr. O'Hara," she said woefully, "I don't know. Nancy's my friend and I love her . . . but I honestly just don't know."

CHAPTER SIX

*S*HE HAD AWAKENED to an inky blackness, with an aching head and the foul, nauseating smell of chloroform clinging to her. She was gagged, and when she tried to move she found her wrists and ankles bound. Dear God, she thought in stunned disbelief, I have been kidnapped! I, Nancy Ryan, have been kidnapped. And she knew that some terrible, idiotic mistake had been made. This couldn't be happening, not to her. But you're not Nancy Ryan now, she told herself, you're Nancy Webster. And David's family is wealthy and David loves you, and that is why you have been abducted.

But almost as incredible, as fantastic, was that her kidnapper was Andy Fisher. Andy, who had never given a damn about money, never given a damn about anything in all his life except his gardens. As a kid she had tagged after him all over the village, hero-worshipping him for the magic things he could do with flowers. He knew everything about them. He even knew their Latin names, and he had taught them to her. He had been sweet and shy and very kind; they had been friends. What in God's name could have happened to gentle Andy Fisher that he should have bound and gagged her, and kidnapped her, and taken her . . . where? Where *had* he taken her. Where was she?

She knew that she was in the back of his pickup truck, covered with something—a blanket, maybe, or a tarpaulin—so thick that she couldn't tell if it was night or day. She could feel the cold hard metal that she was lying on, and there was the smell of the earth and fertilizer and seaweed that he stacked in his truck to spread on his gardens all over the town.

The truck was not moving, but there was a sort of swaying motion, a throbbing, that she did not recognize until she heard the shrill blasts of the fog horns, and realized that she was on the island ferry. In a few minutes she felt the ship slow down as it nudged into the slip. All around her she could hear cars being started. And then the pickup was moving over the ramp, out onto the dock, and she knew she was on land. But whether she was in Woods Hole on the mainland, or out in the Atlantic Ocean on the island of Nantucket, she had no idea.

Police Officer Al Potter was driving the patrol car down Main Street when he saw Ken Lambert turn into School Street, obviously on his way to the *Gazette* office. Potter was reminded that the Chief had asked him to take up a police matter with Lambert. The reason the Chief had asked him to do it, instead of doing it himself, was that it had been Potter's idea. By the time he drove around the block, parked the car, and went into the newspaper office, Lambert was settled down at his typewriter.

"Ken," Potter said, "there's something you can do for us—write for us."

"Sure, anything. Almost."

"About the break-ins at the houses closed for the winter. You with me?"

"Right with you."

"Well, we got two more reports on break-ins. Summer people coming out to the island for a weekend and discovering their houses have been broken into and robbed."

"That makes about seven or eight."

"Eleven," Potter said. "It's been happening all fall. I've got a theory about it. Nothing valuable was taken at most of the houses. Of course when the summer people close their places, they don't leave money, jewelry, the Mona Lisa, or negotiable stocks and bonds lying around all winter. But they *do* leave TV sets and hi-fis, radios—things like that. But in most of the houses nothing was stolen. Except, if there was any around, liquor."

"And there usually was some liquor around," Ken said, grinning.

"There was some in every house but one," Potter said, grinning back. "Shame on those summer people."

"Bad as some of us winter people," Ken said.

"Present company excepted, of course. The house that didn't have any liquor—nothing was taken. The place had been broken into, all right, but nothing was gone. Get it?"

"Yeah. Those thieves were after liquor, but not anything else."

Potter nodded. "And I can go a step further than that. They can't afford to buy it. They have to steal."

"That follows," Ken said.

"And at several places we found bicycle tracks, different sets of them. More kids ride bikes than adults—"

"Oh, Lord," Ken said. "It's kids who are breaking into

45

houses, stealing liquor? Is that what you're suggesting?"

"That's it."

"Damn it, I don't like to think we have teenagers here who—"

"Ken, in this country there are grade school kids who are drug addicts. You know that."

"Yes, but I was thinking only of the Vineyard. We've got teenage kids here maybe turning into alcoholics? Well, sure, let's face it, of course we could have. But I'm hoping you're wrong."

"Do you think I hope I'm right?" Potter said. "But I'm afraid I am."

"Look, adults *do* ride bikes."

"I got more than that, Ken. The last place that got hit was the Friedlander's house. They came up a couple of weeks ago to spend a few days and found some liquor gone. Also missing was a stack of their kid's comic books."

"Comic books! Jesus! Maybe not teenagers, maybe even younger," Ken said, and sighed. "So that's the story you want me to write."

"Yeah. Write about the break-ins again. Mention the stolen liquor and the missing comic books. Say that we could be making an arrest soon."

"Could you be?"

"No, but we're hoping the kids, whoever they are, will read or hear about the story, and get scared off."

"You think they'll give up stealing liquor?" Ken asked.

"And maybe give up drinking liquor."

"Yeah, that's just as important," Ken said. "Well, I'll do my best."

"It'll be in tomorrow's paper?"

"Yes. I'll write it now." Ken shook his head. "You know, I turned down big city jobs with all their lousy problems and stayed here so I wouldn't have to write this kind of lousy story."

46

"The Barrow trial was pretty rough," Potter said. "You covered that."

"I guess it's true," Ken said. "There's no place left to hide."

David Webster was confused as he paced around the big empty house, going out on the front steps every now and then to look down Water Street, hoping to see headlights, and then a small red car come and turn into the drive. A number of cars had passed, but none of them had been the red Mercedes.

He had been puzzled that there had been no Nancy at the airport and, when he called home, that there had been no answer. And still more puzzled, after a taxi had dropped him at the house, to find it locked and empty, and Mrs. Mac's car in the garage and Nancy's gone. But he hadn't worried. He had figured there were any number of logical explanations, and at any minute either the phone would ring, and it would be Nancy explaining, or Nancy would arrive home to deliver her logical explanation in person.

He was in the kitchen when the phone finally did ring and he answered it there.

"I have a collect call for you," the operator said, "from Pocasset, from Nancy. Will you accept the charges?"

He said he would of course accept the charges, and then he heard Nancy's voice. "Dave? Oh, Dave—"

"Nancy! What's happening? What the hell are you doing over on the Cape?"

"I've been kidnapped, I—"

"You've been . . . what did you say?"

"I've been kidnapped. I've been told exactly what to say to you, Dave. And I'm to tell you there's a knife being held at my side while I say it. Can you hear me?"

"Yes," he said. "Yes, I can hear you."

"He—the kidnapper wants a hundred thousand dollars. In fifty and one hundred dollar bills. He will give you until tomorrow night to get it. He wants you to be home then, and he will contact you."

"I'll be here," David said. "I'll have the money. Tell him I'll be here and I'll have his goddamn money."

He says that if you call the police, the F.B.I.—anything like that—I'll be killed. he says he means it, Dave."

"Nancy, I promise I won't call the police! Tell him I *swear* I'll do everything he asks!"

"Dave . . . oh, darling—"

The line went dead. Either the kidnapper had broken the connection or, David thought grimly, he had suggested that Nancy break it, by drawing a drop or two of her blood.

She felt him increase the sharp pressure of the knife, then relax a little as she obeyed his whispered order to hang up the phone. But immediately, as the lights of a passing car flashed across the booth, the pressure returned. When the car's taillights had faded, Andy pushed her out the door.

"All right," he said. "Come on, now."

While she had been talking to David she had used her free hand to stealthily tug off the silk scarf she was wearing, and roll it into a small ball. Now, before Andy closed the door and the booth went dark, she dropped it on the ground behind her. Andy took one step, then stopped; and for a moment she thought he had seen what she had done. But he had merely halted to look in all directions before, the knife once more jabbing her,

48

they started down the road to where he had left the truck.

There was, she thought ruefully, little need for his caution. He had chosen the place for the phone call well. The tiny business district of this small summer resort town was completely deserted. The phone booth they had used stood outside a closed garage, across the street from a motel that was closed for the winter. The other buildings that lined the street—souvenir shops, a second-hand bookstore, several seafood eateries, a bicycle rental shop, and other stores providing the necessities for summer vacationers—were shuttered. The street lights were far apart and dim. It seemed to Nancy as though she and her kidnapper were the only creatures stirring in this cold dark village by the sea. She shivered as the brisk wind raced through the street, and turned her jacket collar up, praying that Andy wouldn't notice that her scarf was gone.

She didn't really dare hope that dropping it at the phone booth would come to anything, but at least she'd done something. In fact, she thought ironically, it was traditional. In almost every kidnap story or film she had read or seen, the victim had always left a trail for the hero—or a private detective or the F.B.I.—for someone on the good guys' side to follow. So maybe someone would find her scarf, and maybe, by some miracle, trace it to her and contact David. And he would follow her this far. And if somehow she could keep on leaving clues, wherever they might go, perhaps by some further miracle she would be rescued. No, that was asking too much. But it was a good thought, a comforting one. It was a thought she would try to hold on to.

Then she heard a voice calling out behind her, and then footsteps running in their direction. The knife jabbed a warning.

"Don't stop, don't look back," Andy told her. "Just keep on walking."

His grasp tightened on her arm and he pulled her forward with him, almost running now, his limp becoming more pronounced, his gait stumbling and crablike. Nancy found it almost impossible to keep in step with him. The footsteps behind them were still coming on, and a woman's voice called down the empty street.

"Hey you! Wait! Wait a minute, for heaven's sake!"

For a moment more Andy reeled on, but the woman kept on running, closing in on them. He had no choice but to stop. Clutching Nancy close to him, chin buried in his coat collar, cap brim pulled down low over his eyes, he turned toward the woman who stood, gasping for breath, before them. They were so far from a street lamp, the light was so dim, that Nancy could only see that the woman was short and stout, an almost shapeless figure in a bulky sweater and slacks. She was holding something dangling from her outstretched hand.

"I'm doing you a favor, for heaven's sake," the fat woman said, still panting. "I saw you drop your scarf at the phone booth back there."

Nancy took the silk scarf and draped it around her neck. The razor-sharp knife nudged her—menacing her, warning her.

"Thank you," she said. "It was very good of you...."

Beside her Andy muttered something inaudible. Then he jerked her around, away from the woman, and once again, locked together, they lurched along the road. There was no further sound from the woman, but glancing back, Nancy saw her standing in the street, staring after them. Oh, thank you very much, you nice fat lady, she thought, but that was no favor you did me.

50

Far from it. But then it probably couldn't have mattered less.

"You did that on purpose, didn't you? Dropping that scarf." Still forcing her hurriedly along in their clumsy waddle, Andy snatched it from her neck. "Well, you won't do anything like that again. I'll see to that."

CHAPTER SEVEN

SABRA MACWILLIAMS and her dear friend Frieda Cass had much in common. They were colleagues. Both were housekeepers, both were widows, and all two of them like an occasional drink. They had spent an eminently successful afternoon shopping in Hyannis, Christmas shopping, and they were justifiably pleased with themselves for having done it so early. But that was the way these two elderly New England islanders had been brought up; a stitch in time saves nine, good fences make good neighbors, do your Christmas shopping early.

Frieda and Sabra were a little too pleased with themselves for their own good. Before a delicious seafood dinner at a Hyannis restaurant they had celebrated their early Christmas shopping with several occasional dry Martinis. With dinner they shared a bottle of white wine. And after dinner they enjoyed a few stingers, telling each other that it was too bad that Christmas came only once a year.

Somehow Frieda managed to steer her old Studebaker safely as far as Falmouth. But on the road to Woods Hole, concerned for their safety, Sabra felt called upon to criticize her friend's driving.

"Don't look now, Frieda," she said, "but you're on the wrong side of the road."

"Don't be so fussy. What's wrong with this side?"

"Well, there's a big truck coming straight at us."

"Oh, yes! Thanks." Frieda got out of the way of the approaching truck. "Missed me by a mile!"

"You better let me drive," Sabra said.

"We'll both drive," Frieda said. "Scrunch over."

"All right," Sabra said. She scrunched herself over, closer to the steering wheel. "Good idea."

Indeed, it worked out well. Frieda's tendency this evening was to veer to the left, Sabra's to the right. Together they arrived unscathed at the dock in Woods Hole, just as the last cars were boarding the ferry. Together they managed a wobbling drive up the gang-plank and to park in the hold.

"You know," Frieda said, applying her brakes belatedly and only slightly denting the car ahead of her, fortunately already empty, "we shouldn't be driving. Neither of us."

"You're right," Sabra said. "We're in no condition to drive."

"We could get arrested for drunken driving. And fined."

"And get our name in the *Gazette* for everybody to see. But what can we do, Frieda?"

"Let's go up and get some coffee and figure something out."

As they worked their way unsteadily through the rows of cars they came to a blue pickup truck. Frieda looked in at the driver's window, Sabra, the one opposite. They said, "Well, hello there, Andy!" They knew they wouldn't have to figure out what to do after all.

"Hello, Mrs. MacWilliams," Andy Fisher said. "Hello, Mrs. Cass."

Frieda stuck her head in the window. "Andy," she said, giggling, "you want to know something?"

Andy didn't answer.

"You promise you won't tell anybody?"

Still Andy didn't answer.

"We've had too much to drink. We're drunk!" Frieda announced. "We're drunk as a skunk!"

"Both of us. Two skunks." Sabra said, sticking her head in the other window. "Too drunk to drive."

"So if you'll drive us home in your truck," Frieda said, "we'll be very, very grateful."

"And we'll pay you," Sabra said.

"No," Andy said. "No."

"Why, Andy," Frieda said, completely surprised, "you wouldn't want us to get arrested, would you?"

"And fined?" Sabra said. "And get our names in the paper and be mortified?"

"I won't drive you," Andy said, between clenched teeth. "I won't do it."

"Andy," Sabra said, "we're old friends. You've always been—"

He rolled up the window on Sabra's side, then rolled up the one on Frieda's side. The two ladies were flabbergasted. Silently, each one helping the other more than was actually necessary, they made their way up to the upper deck. There they ordered coffee, black and strong.

"That Andy," Frieda said. "Not like him to act like that. Not like him at all."

"Strange," Sabra said. "That's what it was. Downright *strange* of Andy."

Four years ago Mr. Henry Jacoby, one of the bigger Madison Avenue advertising wheels, had given his Dorothy a birthday present. Overwhelmed, she could not thank him enough for it; it had been a house on Cooke Street. By then Dorothy had become disenchanted with New York City, even occasionally frightened by it. Then last spring Henry had given her another present for which she was, if possible, even more grateful. He had decided to take early retirement. He had put their condominium on East Seventy-ninth on the market, promptly sold it at a large profit, and told Dorothy he would be glad to live with her on the island all year round.

"Dottie," he had said to her, "you need never see New York City again."

"I would love that, thank you very much," she had answered. "And from now on I will love you more than ever."

"I doubt, dear, if that is possible," he had said with a smile. "But please feel free to try."

So now Mr. and Mrs. Henry Jacoby were spending their first winter on the island of their choice. This evening, in front of a blazing fire of pine logs, which he had culled, gratis, with his chain saw from the State Forest nearby, Dottie was getting rid of her last New-York-City-related item—apart from, of course, her husband. It was a Saks Fifth Avenue shoe box filled with old letters, recipes, newspaper and magazine clippings, and other odds and ends. Henry was sitting in his favorite chair, having a nightcap and avidly studying the stack of seed catalogues he had sent away for. For the last four years Andy Fisher had taken care of the garden for them, and of the closed-up house during the winter, but this spring Henry was going to be his own gardener, growing flowers and vegetables.

"Dottie, listen to this!" he said. "A new thing called snap peas. You can eat the pods and all. Won the guy who developed it a prize. Sounds great, doesn't it?"

"Um . . . sounds positively yummy," Dottie said. "Grow bushels. We'll freeze some."

"Freeze well," Henry read from his catalogue, "can poorly."

"I hate to can," Dottie said, working on her shoe box. "Love to freeze."

She glanced over two Craig Claiborne recipes she had clipped years ago from the *New York Times,* and still had not tried. She decided to keep the one for *Moussaka à la Grecque;* she put it aside. The one for a chocolate mousse torte she crumpled and tossed into the fire. She and Henry had both resolved to go on diets.

"If you'll grow some eggplant, darling," she said, "I've got a good recipe here for moussaka."

"Would you believe it?" Henry said. "I'm on that page right now. 'Eggplant . . . Burpee's Black Beauty, seventy-four days. Tender and tasty at all stages of growth.' I'll have to start them in the greenhouse."

"We don't have a greenhouse, dear."

"Not yet," Henry said, "but we will in plenty of time."

"My oh my," Dottie said. "My husband the gardener, complete with his very own greenhouse."

"You bet, love."

Now Dottie came upon an old clipping from the *Vineyard Gazette.* It was dated November, three years ago. She glanced at it briefly and was puzzled. It was a continued-from-page-one story about the Barrow murder case. She hadn't been on the island when that happened; she wondered who could have sent it to her in New York, and why. She flipped it over and found the answer.

On the other side was an article about island birds, and about the annual Christmas count. Dottie was an enthusiastic bird watcher, and she remembered now that it had been sent to her from the island by another devout bird watcher, Marion Weaver. Well, news of a long past Christmas count was nothing to keep around, and she threw it into the fire. She watched it burn, thinking maybe she should have saved it, but not knowing why.

A few minutes later the shoebox was empty. It joined its former contents in the flames, and she watched it blaze. When nothing remained but white ashes, she said softly, "Oh, damn it!"

"Damn what?" Henry asked, still deep in his catalogues.

"Oh, a clipping about the Barrow murder case that I just burned. It was on the back of a bird count thing that Marion Weaver sent me. Strange, I don't remember ever seeing that story about the murder until tonight."

"Well, what about it?"

"I didn't actually read it, I just skipped over it, so I don't really know. But something about it bothers me—and I can't think what."

"Tomorrow morning I'll ask you what bothered you, and then, refreshed by a good night's sleep, you'll think of it."

"Don't forget to ask me. Well, I think I'll join you for a nightcap, and then it's bed for me."

"May I join you there?"

"Need you ask?" Dottie said. "Welcome aboard."

Andy looked at his watch. In a matter of minutes, in spite of the fog, they would be landing. That was none too soon for him. He had thought he was so safe up here in the cab of his truck. Then the two old ladies had appeared so suddenly, so unexpectedly, looming up at both his windows like a pair of vultures, trapping him between them. His throat had tightened, dried up on him, he had barely been able to answer them.

Now the deckhands were pulling open the great double steel doors, and Andy could see the lights of Vineyard Haven glimmering through the fog. He had made it, he told himself, all fears allayed. Taking Nancy over on the ferry had been the most dangerous part of his plan, but it was worth it. The toll call coming from Pocasset would prove that she was off-island. If David went to the police—Andy was certain he wouldn't—but *if* he did, they would go looking for her all over the Cape, never dreaming she was right here on the Vineyard. Oh, that was smart of him. Risky, but smart. And now that part of it was over. From here on in it would be plain sailing.

His pickup was in one of the two center lanes, and only third in line. If his luck held, his lane would be the first one off. It didn't matter though. The boat was less than half full, no more than twenty cars on it. Even if his lane was last to go, it wouldn't take long.

Its engines throbbing in reverse, the ferry nudged into the slip and was secured at its moorings. The stairway to the upper deck was unchained, and the scattering of late-night foot passengers trudged wearily down the steps and onto the dock. A deckhand motioned to the lane next to Andy's. Motors started up, headlights were turned on, and the cars began rolling off the ship.

The car at the head of Andy's lane, at a signal from the deckhand, started to move. Andy switched on his ignition, and nothing happened. The motor did not turn over. He stared at the unlighted dashboard in disbelief. Frantically, he switched on his windshield wipers, pounded his fist on the horn. Still nothing happened, and he knew in a wave of rage and frustration that his battery was dead.

The driver behind him honked his horn, angry at missing his turn to go home, as the deckhand moved to another lane of cars, signalling it to get going. Fighting down his rising panic, Andy watched the cars in the other lanes drive quickly off the boat, their taillights disappearing as they reached the dock. The deckhand was motioning to the cars trapped behind him, and they backed up and pulled into the adjacent empty lane. Going past him, their drivers sent him looks of disgust.

His pickup was the last vehicle left on the boat, and three deckhands were coming toward him. He knew two of them; Fred Nelson and Tony Marcos, they had been in school with him. They were calling his name, laughing at him, asking him what was the matter. When he said his battery was dead, they told him to put the truck in neutral and they would push him off.

His hands were shaking so badly, were so slippery with sweat, he could hardly manage to shift gears. When the truck started to move it took every ounce of strength he had merely to hold onto the wheel. In the rearview mirror he could see the three men, their hands on his tailgate, only inches from the tarp that was covering Nancy. Laughing, they made a great show of pushing with all their might; in a moment the truck was rolling by itself, leaving the deckhands behind. With a shudder of relief Andy steered the pickup into an empty taxi parking slot. Quickly he jumped out of the cab and raised the hood, praying that the deckhands would join him there; that they would walk around the body of his truck without glancing into it.

He heard the deckhand he didn't know calling good night to the other two. Then Tony and Fred, still laughing, came to stand beside Andy.

Hastily, before they had a chance to speak, Andy said, "You can charge my battery for me, can't you, Fred? You got a booster in your car."

"Me?" Fred said. "I got a booster in my car? What's a booster, Andy?"

"Please," Andy pleaded, "don't make jokes. I'm tired. I don't feel good."

"You don't look sick to me," Fred said. "Does he look sick to you, Tony?"

"No," Tony said, "Andy don't look sick to me. I never saw him looking better."

"On second thought," Fred said, "he don't look so good to me. Maybe we should rush him to the hospital."

"Oh, please," Andy said, "oh, please, Fred. I know you got a booster. I saw you using it on someone's car just last week."

"Yeah, Mrs. Winston's car. But I sold it yesterday. Look, Andy, it's only about ten miles to your place. Why don't you walk home the ten miles and in the morning walk back the ten miles, and I'll borrow back the booster. Will you loan me back the booster, Fred?"

Tony laughed, but he said, "Let's knock it off now, huh, Fred?"

"Sure, I'll knock it off and I'll get Andy my booster," Fred said, "if first Andy will tell me something. Will you tell me something, Andy?"

"Yes," he said desperately. "Anything."

"I seen something move in the back of your pickup," Fred said. "Under the tarp."

Through stiff lips Andy said, "Under the tarp?"

"What you got under there anyway?"

"Some more rabbits, what else?" Tony said. "Right, Andy? You buy yourself some more rabbits?"

"Yes, that's right," Andy said fervidly. "A pair of Belgians."

"You get them at Buzz Campbell's place?" Tony asked.

"Sure, I always buy there."

"Listen, Andy," Fred said, "what I want to know is—"

"Oh, come on," Tony said. When Fred Nelson got his hands on his idea of a joke, he never let go. "It's getting late. Let's get Andy going."

"Okay."

In less than five minutes the battery had been charged and the blue pickup was rolling through the night.

CHAPTER EIGHT

*I*T WAS A FEW minutes after eleven o'clock when Sabra MacWilliams arrived at the house on Water Street. Her friend Frieda had driven so carefully, so slowly, from the ferry, by the time they reached Edgartown they were both sober. Sabra didn't have to use her key; the front door was unlocked. There were lights on in several downstairs rooms, but the house seemed strangely quiet. She found David in the library, standing at the window.

"Hello, David, welcome home. Have a good trip?"

He turned to her. He didn't have to say anything. She could tell from his face that something disastrous had happened.

"Dave, what is it? Is it Nancy" And she knew it had to be Nancy. Nothing else could have made him look like that.

"She's been kidnapped," he said.

For a moment Mrs. MacWilliams thought that she might faint. Her vision blurred, and she felt weak and giddy. She held tightly to the back of a chair. Then with a great effort she got hold of herself. She was a Yankee, a tough old bird, and not the fainting kind. She might be needed. She hoped to God she would be needed.

She said, "David, tell me."

"She called from Pocasset. She told me the kidnapper was holding a knife on her. He wants a hundred thousand dollars. They will contact me here tomorrow night."

"Can you get it—the money? By tomorrow night?"

"Yes. I've talked to my father. I can get it tomorrow morning in Boston."

"Thank God."

"I've got a seat on the nine o'clock plane; I think I can get the one o'clock back. And while I'm gone, Mrs. Mac, I'm counting on you."

"Anything, David."

"If the police find out, if anyone does, Nancy said he would kill her. She says the kidnapper means it."

"Oh, dear God," Mrs. MacWilliams said.

"You and I, Mrs. Mac, and Dad, are the only ones who know. We've got to keep it that way. While I'm off-island tomorrow you'll have to carry on here by yourself."

"I'll do anything you say."

"Nancy's sick, she's staying in bed for a day or two. That's what you'll tell anyone who wants to see her. Or talk to her on the phone. Say it's nothing serious, just a cold, a sore throat, that's why she can't talk to anyone. You understand, don't you?"

"Yes. And I'll manage, David, I promise you."

"I know you will. Try to get some sleep tonight, Mrs. Mac, or at least some rest. We may have some very rough days ahead of us."

Timothy O'Hara turned on his bed lamp to see how long he had been tossing and turning. Twenty minutes past eleven. Almost an effing hour. But why should he complain? Because of his bad legs, tossing and turning was about all the exercise he got nowadays. But it would be great to go to bed and immediately fall asleep. To sleep like a log. He couldn't remember the last time he had slept like a log. You hardly ever saw a tired log. He decided he would try counting sheep.

Switching off the lamp, he counted nine sheep while tossing once, then thought about his scheduled call tomorrow morning to make a progress report to Andrews. He had no progress to report. Three effing days on the job and no progress whatsoever to report. At the moment, it didn't much look like he was going to prove that Nancy Webster was innocent of the murder of her first husband. It looked more like Andrews's sneaky strategy to prove O'Hara's incompetence and justify his immediate retirement would be effective.

God help him, what would he do if he retired? He wasn't in good enough shape to enjoy retirement. He couldn't go to Florida and play golf or even shuffleboard. Just standing still, doing nothing, hurt. He couldn't take long walks, or go sight-seeing, or garden . . . was there anything he could do outdoors? And him an old outdoors man. Well, he cold retire to Florida and take his television out on the patio. But, no, thanks. Not that.

He could visit his daughter Irene for two weeks every year. She might be able to stand him for that long. Irene had married into the U.S. Navy, and was now in San Diego, raising four kids. He wished that Marjorie could have lived to see her four grandchildren. Well, at least she had still been around to see her darling daughter happily married.

In San Diego he would have to sleep on a sofa in the living room, but he guessed he could stand that for two weeks every year. But what would he do with the other fifty? Why did there have to be fifty-two effing weeks in every year?

He had an out. Solve this case. Prove that he was still a competent operator. Keep his job, which his effing legs could still manage to do. Lately it had been his effing brain, not just his effing legs, that had failed him.

Get some sleep, you old Irish fool, O'Hara told himself, and tomorrow be brilliant. Crack the case, keep your job, save a lovely young woman's future. Good night, Timothy O'Hara, and good luck to you. And to you, Nancy Webster.

He tossed and he turned.

Didn't sleep like a log.

Worried.

Halfway through Katama the blue pickup truck turned off the paved road to South Beach and onto a dirt one that soon split three ways. The truck jounced along the middle road, through some heavy woods of stunted pine and oak, then climbed sharply to a bluff that overlooked the bay, and stopped before a huge, sprawling house of weathered shingle.

The Goldsmith house was the most remote of the eight or nine places where Andy was employed as gardener in the summer and caretaker in the winter. Now, in November, there wasn't an occupied house within a mile of it. It was strictly a summer house, with no central heating. There was no chance of the Goldsmiths dropping in unexpectedly for a weekend. They spent their winters in Arizona. Andy knew the Goldsmith house was a good place, the best place, for what he had to do.

He got out of his truck and waited for a moment instinctively, listening. The fog had dissolved. There was no sound. No wind, no surf. Nothing. He looked up at the cloudless sky, picking out a few of his favorite stars. Then he went quickly to work. First he climbed the few steps up to the veranda and unlocked the front door. Using his pencil flashlight, he went into the house where he lit the candles he had placed on the coffee table the night before. The electric power had been turned off for the winter. Last night, after lighting the candles, he had drawn the drapes over all the windows, then gone outside to circle the house, making certain that no glimmer of light could be seen by anyone passing by. He knew that nobody would be passing anywhere near the place, not this time of year, but he wasn't taking any chances at all.

Leaving the front door open, he went back to the truck and lifted the tarpaulin off Nancy. He folded it carefully and stored it beneath the seat. His hands on her ankles, he drew her to him across the ingate. He lifted her against his chest and carried her into the house. In the big living room he lowered her onto a sofa. Then he went outside again, drove his truck across the frozen lawn, and parked it behind a dilapidated old carriage house, where it was hidden from view.

Back in the house he looked down at Nancy and saw that she was awake and shivering; the house was even colder than the night outside. He picked up a blanket that he had taken from a bedroom the night before, and tucked it around her.

"Are you hungry, Nancy?" he asked. "You want something to eat?"

Furiously, she shook her head.

"You didn't have any supper," he said. "I laid in some stuff. I got peanut butter and bologna. I could make you some real nice sandwiches." He remembered that when she was little she used to especially like bologna sandwiches. Sometimes when he was working at the Ryan house she would make sandwiches for both of them, and they would have a picnic in the garden. He had really enjoyed those times they spent together. "Should I make you some sandwiches, Nancy? You've got to eat something."

He reached down and ripped the electrical tape from her mouth, and then her pent up anger exploded.

"No, I do not want a sandwich! I want to know why you are doing this to me! A hundred thousand dollars, Andy! Why do you want all that money, for God's sake! What will you do with it?"

He didn't answer her. She saw the stubbornness in his eyes and she knew that her anger was having no effect on him. She steadied herself, quieted her voice.

"Look, Andy," she said. "Whatever you want it for, this is no way to get it. There's some other way—"

"No," he said, "this is the way it's got to be."

"No, it hasn't! Remember you're my old pal, my old, dear, friend. You haven't hurt me, you never would. We can forget this ever happened and I'll see you get your money, I promise you."

"It isn't just the money," Andy said. "I'm not doing this just for the money."

"Then why? *Why* are you doing it?"

He looked at her gravely. "To punish you," he said. "I'm doing it to punish you for the terrible thing you did to me."

"To you? What did I do? For God's sake, Andy, tell me what I did!"

"You told me that you loved me," he said in a sullen voice. "You used to follow me all around, give me hugs and kisses. You said when you grew up you were going to marry me. You promised. Remember, Nancy?"

67

"Andy, I was a *child!* I was five or six years old!"

"But you loved me," he said stubbornly. "Even when you stopped following me around, and hugging me, I knew it wasn't because you didn't love me anymore. It was because your mother and father wouldn't let you. Even after I pushed you away from that truck they didn't like me, not really. Not enough to let us be together. They kept us apart. It was their fault, not yours."

"Oh, dear God. . . ."

"I understood. I knew you didn't want to hurt them. But I always knew that you would come to me as soon as you could. And when they died, I waited for you. I thought you would come back to the island, and marry me, and I would take care of you for the rest of your life. But when you did come, it wasn't to me. You came back with a husband. So what I did was all for nothing."

He saw the horror fill Nancy's eyes.

"Yes," he told her, "I did it, Nancy. I killed your mother and father. I blew up their boat."

CHAPTER NINE

*B*Y NINE O'CLOCK on this gray November morning, Timothy O'Hara was sitting in the living room of the Winston house on Cooke Street, talking with Ethel Winston. She was a delightful looking woman in her mid-fifties, with a trim, girlish figure, short-cropped silver-gray curls and, O'Hara thought, the bluest eyes he had ever seen.

"On that terrible evening," she was saying to him, "I was in the kitchen making a dessert for a dinner party I was having the next night. I remember every damn thing about it. I was dissolving some gelatin and I had just set the timer on the stove clock. That's how I know it was *exactly* nine thirty when I saw Nancy."

"Your kitchen window looks out on the Barrow house," O'Hara said.

Ethel smiled. "We still call it the Ryan house, Mr. O'Hara. It's an island quirk. My husband and I bought this house from the Lindstroms in 1960, but it wasn't till years later, after my husband died, that people stopped calling it the damn Lindstrom house and admitted it was the damn Winston place. But, yes, the window does look out on the Ryan house—come, let me show you."

In the kitchen the smell of breakfast coffee was still bracingly strong, and Ethel caught O'Hara sniffing it with appreciation.

"Would you like a cup, Mr. O'Hara?"

"No, thank you," he said regretfully. "It makes me want a cigarette."

"How about a doughnut?" Ethel suggested. "Or would it make you want a cup of coffee?"

O'Hara laughed, declined the doughnut, and got down to business. "You saw Nancy from this window?"

Ethel nodded. "I was at the sink there, and I saw her bending over the flower box next to the door."

"It was dark—after nine o'clock."

"There's a street light. I could see her, and the flower box, quite clearly."

"But you couldn't actually see what she was doing, could you?"

The blue eyes clouded over. "No, not really," she said. "Her back was to me, but I got the impression that she was digging in the box. I thought it was crazy she would be doing that at night, with the earth frozen solid."

"How long did you watch her?"

"For exactly three minutes."

"You're certain of that, Mrs. Winston?"

"Yes," she said unhappily, "I'm dead certain."

"If I remember her testimony correctly," O'Hara said, "Nancy said she wasn't at the box for more than a second or two. She said when she got home the door was locked. She rang, but her husband didn't answer. So she went to the flower box to get a key she kept hidden there, under the dead leaves. She said she found it right away. In a few seconds."

Ethel nodded. "Yes, and if I had known that's what she was going to tell the police, it's what I would have

70

told them, too. But they asked me before I knew that. And I told them what I saw, what I honestly thought I saw."

"You mean," O'Hara asked curiously, "you would have perjured yourself to help Nancy?"

"I would have done anything," Edthel Winston said. "She's a very special young person. I would have done a lot more than tell the police a lie if it would have helped her. And if I had, then Nancy and I might still be friends."

"You're no longer friends?"

"No, I'm afraid not," Ethel said. "When I heard that she and David were back I went over to see her, to welcome her home. But it wasn't the same. I know she still blames me for telling the police what I did. I don't see how she can ever forgive me for that."

"How can you be so certain you were right, Mrs. Winston? About the time?"

Suddenly Ethel Winston was angry. "Because of that goddamn stove timer. I had set it for three minutes, just before I looked out the window and saw Nancy. She was still standing over the box when it buzzed. After I turned it off I looked out the window again, and she was gone. But, damn it, I watched her here for exactly three minutes."

"Yes. Plenty long enough to bury a gun," O'Hara said, discouraged. "Sorry to have upset you so, Mrs. Winston."

She shok her head emphatically. "It didn't take you to upset me, Mr. O'Hara. I'll never get over what I did to Nancy."

Andy Fisher quickly finished checking up on the Jenner house on Atwood Circle, a job he did six days a

71

week all through the winter months, and started across town to the Davallion place on Fuller Street. There was a lot of work to be done there, not just going through the house. The yard needed his attention. The roses around the terrace needed to be pruned, the lawn could use one last mowing. There were the dahlia bulbs to be dug up and stored in the cellar for the winter. The Davallion house would take him the rest of the morning, maybe part of the afternoon. Nevertheless, the route he took there was a circuitous one.

He drove slowly, but not noticeably so, up and down several streets, letting himself be seen, waving back to anyone who waved at him. He was acting real natural, doing today just like what he did every day, as though he didn't have Nancy Ryan locked up in the Goldsmith house, bound hand and foot.

He drove along Church Street past the police station. Everything seemed normal there. There were no strange cars in the parking space, no State Police or mainland patrol cars. He also noticed that all the Edgartown policemen who were supposed to be on duty in the morning were on the streets. He was relieved to see that David Webster certainly couldn't have said anything to the cops.

On Main Street as he passed the town hall, he slowed down so he could see what was playing at the movie theatre on the second floor. Andy loved the movies. He never missed going on Saturday nights, hadn't since he was a kid. He went every time they changed the picture, too, sometimes several times a week.

He saw that the picture playing on Friday and Saturday night was one he had seen before. Twice before, in fact. It didn't matter. It was a darned good movie, he had liked it a lot. And no matter what was playing the place was always crowded on Saturday night, so that would be all right.

When he got to Water Street he turned left and from there he drove straight to the Davallion house on Fuller Street. He parked the pickup in the driveway, then went into the garage and wheeled out the lawn mower. The first thing he would do was give the grass its last cutting. It was best for a lawn not to be more than two inches high over the winter.

The phone rang at ten that morning, and Mrs. Mac-Williams went quickly into the library to answer it. While David was gone she was in charge of guarding the secret they shared, and she dreaded hearing the phone ring or the doorbell sound.

"Hello, Mrs. MacWilliams," a voice said. It was a familiar voice, but one that she didn't recognize at once. "May I speak with Dave?"

"I'm afraid he's in Boston this morning," she said. "Who is this, please?"

"It's Jimmy Corto, Mrs. Mac."

"Oh, of course!" she said. Jimmy was a Vineyard boy, he and David had been long-time summer friends. He'd been off-island for several years, but recently he'd come back. In fact, she'd seen him just a week or two ago and, remembering where she had seen him, she sank into the chair beside the desk. He had been in one of the blue and white patrol cars, wearing the uniform of the Edgartown police. Could the police already know about the kidnapping? What in heaven's name should she tell him? How could she handle this?

"Mrs. MacWilliams," Jimmy Corto was saying. "Are you there, Mrs. Mac?"

"Yes, Jimmy."

"Maybe I could talk to Nancy?"

"To . . . Nancy?" She felt the relief pouring through her, her strength returning. The police knew nothing after all. "She can't come to the phone right now, Jimmy. She isn't feeling well."

"Oh, I'm sorry."

"It's nothing serious, just a bad cold. Is there something I can do?"

"Well, it's about her car, the red Mercedes. We found it this morning out at Clam Bay. It hadn't been reported missing or stolen."

"Oh, no, of course it wasn't stolen!" She laughed a bit to give herself a moment to think. Then she said carefully, improvising as she went. "Yes, Clam Bay. . . . Nancy drove out there to take a walk on the beach. When she got back to the car it wouldn't start, or maybe it was out of gas. I don't remember."

"Plenty of gas," Jimmy Corto said. "Trouble was the rotor had been taken out."

"Well," Mrs. MacWilliams said, laughing again, "Nancy wouldn't know anything about rotors. I suppose some of the wild kids we have here nowadays must have done it as a joke!"

"Probably," Jimmy said.

"Anyway, Nancy just left the car there and walked home."

"She didn't get a lift?"

"No, I don't think so. Why?"

"Some other car tracks there, near hers, and footprints. We thought someone must have given her a lift."

"No, I'm sure she said she walked."

"Okay, Mrs. Mac. But what do you want to do about the car? That's a pretty valuable piece of merchandise to be left sitting on the beach."

"David will be home this afternoon, Jimmy. I'll have him take care of it right away. And thanks for calling."

"It's okay, Mrs. Mac. So long."

Mrs. MacWilliams went to the kitchen and stood looking out the window. That morning she had watched a gray and dismal dawn, and the day was continuing dark and gloomy. The weather prediction on the radio had been for rain. She prayed it wouldn't be bad enough to delay David's flight home.

In police headquarters Jimmy Corto put down the telephone and frowned. It could be, as Mrs. Mac had suggested, some mischievous kids who had removed the Mercedes' rotor as a prank. Or it could be a lot nastier; it could be the work of someone who thought the jury should not have acquitted Nancy. Someone who resented the fact that she'd returned to the island.

Henry Jacoby was having his second cup of coffee and glancing occasionally at some midmorning television. His wife joined him with her third cup of tea. She waited for a commercial, then turned down the sound and spoke to her husband.

"Haven't you forgotten something this morning, dear?"

"My God, what? It isn't your birthday, or our anniversary. Or *my* birthday . . . what did I forget?"

"To ask me about the *Gazette* clipping."

"About the Barrow murder, yes. Okay, what bothers you about it?"

"You said I'd know after a good night's sleep."

"And did you get a good night's sleep?"

"Henry, this isn't like not being able to remember a name, or what I wore to the opening of *Forty-Second Street*. This is something about a murder. It's serious!"

"But the trial is long over and done with. And Nancy Barrow was acquitted. So what or who is there for you to worry about?"

"I don't know, damn it. *That's* what worries me. Oh,

it's probably nothing at all. Well. Do you want more coffee?"

"No, thanks, but while you're up, will you turn the sound back on?"

Dottie Jacoby turned the sound back on, but she said, "You don't really listen."

"No, but how can I sincerely not listen if there's no sound?"

Hours ago she had watched the candle sputter and go out, leaving the room in total blackness. Later, a lifetime later, she had seen a hint of gray morning light filter through some window in the hallway, and she had made out the shapes of shouded furniture, and of Andy sitting in a chair close to the cold, dead fireplace. He was motionless, but whether he slept or was watching her she couldn't tell.

He had moved at last; stood up and stretched, and then come to the couch and looked down at her. He had offered her food, but she could only stare up at him in mute horror. He had shrugged, told her he would come back later, and then left her. She had heard the front door close, the click of a key turning in its lock, and a minute later the sound of the pickup truck's motor starting, and the tires on the gravelled drive.

The tape that bound her arms and legs was hurting her. She hardly felt the pain. The house seemed even colder in the sunless day, and she hardly noticed it. After she had emerged from the state of shock into which she had been plunged, she had spent the agonizing hours trying to understand, trying to come to some kind of terms with the horror of the facts confronting her.

Andy Fisher had killed her mother and her father. She

knew without his telling her that he had murdered Jim. And now, for her final punishment, he was going to murder her.

CHAPTER TEN

*T*IMOTHY O'HARA was driving aimlessly around town. Feeling completely at a loss, totally useless, not worth a grain of his salt. Thinking morosely that his boss would be justified in kicking him out into the barren pasture—nay, the dry desert—of retirement. Then, while driving slowly down Main Street past the huge Whalers' Church with its magnificent white columns, and on toward the more modest Catholic church, he had been blessed with help from above. Halfway between those two houses of God he had been hit with an idea.

It wasn't much of an idea, but on second thought, if he was to prove his client's innocence the theory behind his idea had to be correct. If it wasn't correct, Nancy Barrow had probably murdered her husband.

He remembered seeing an outdoor phone booth around the corner, on North Water Street. He parked his car in the nearest space, in front of the library, and walked to the booth more rapidly than he had walked in several years. If his legs were hurting, he didn't notice.

He looked up a number in the phone book chained to the shelf and dialed it. The phone rang three times before Ethel Winston answered it.

"This is Timothy O'Hara," he explained, "the writer fellow. I'm sorry to be bothering you again so soon."

"It's no bother," Ethel protested. "If there's anything I can do, Mr. O'Hara, please tell me."

"It's this," O'Hara said. "I know it was a long time ago, Mrs. Winston, but do you happen to remember what Nancy was wearing the night her husband was murdered? When you saw her at the flower box?"

"Yes, Mr. O'Hara, I do remember."

"Good. That might be of some help to me."

"Help in proving Nancy's innocence?"

"Yes."

"She was wearing a dark scarf around her head, dark slacks. And a yellow jacket."

"Dark scarf and slacks, yellow jacket. Thank you, Mrs. Winston."

"Does that help any?"

"It's too soon to tell."

"Well, if it turns out I have helped—"

"You will be the first to know. I will personally see to that."

She thanked him and hung up. He looked up another number in the phone book and dialed it. He hung on for a long time, listening to the ringing. Mrs. Mickey Jamison was not at home. He called her real estate office and got a busy signal. Well, he would try again, every ten minutes or so.

Walking back to his car he thought of Mrs. Winston and what a pleasant woman she was. And attractive, damn attractive. It had been years since he had noticed that a woman was attractive.

Of all mornings, a disturbed Betty Lou thought, it had to happen this morning! First of all she didn't get a chance to speak privately to Amy Lambert on the school bus. She didn't get a chance in their home room, either, or during classes or between them. And never had she needed so much to speak to her best friend privately. She had to warn Amy. They were headed for big, big trouble.

The last straw for Betty Lou came just before lunch. Out of the blue her English teacher, Miss Byers, asked her to stay for minuter after class, and she wasted five precious minutes complimenting Betty Lou on a short story she had written. Miss Byers thought Betty Lou had imagination and remarkable style for one so young. She encouraged her to write more stories.

Betty Lou promised she would, then hurried to the cafeteria, but she was too late. Amy was already seated at a table with three other girls, happily chattering away as if she didn't have a worry in the world. Little did she know, Betty Lou thought. She snatched up a tray, loaded it hurriedly with macaroni casserole, a carton of milk and a dish of Jello, and headed for Amy's table.

She stopped long enough to whisper into Amy's ear. "Follow me! Urgent! Red alert!"

Amy picked up her tray and followed Betty Lou to an empty table. When they sat down Betty Lou saw that her friend had managed to get herself not only the macaroni casserole but tuna fish salad with potato chips as well, and had already eaten half of each. Obviously, Betty Lou realized, Amy did not know the trouble she was headed for.

"Amy," she said, "you haven't seen today's *Gazette*, have you?"

Amy shook her head.

"Right there on the front page! My father read it to my mother."

"Come on, Betty Lou. What?"

"*Your* father wrote the story. About empty houses being broken into and liquor stolen."

"That's been in the paper before," Amy said.

"But this time it's different. It's scary! The police think kids are doing it. They found bike tire tracks at some of the houses and—"

"We aren't the only kids doing it," Amy said.

"No, but we're two of them. And, Amy, they're sure it's kids. In one of the houses some comic books were taken."

"Comic books!" Amy said disdainfully. "Who in heck would be dumb enough to steal comic books!"

"Well . . . ." Betty Lou said.

"Well, what?"

"Nothing. It's just that I'm scared. I'm not going to do it any more."

"Oh, come on, Betty Lou!"

"No! Not any more!"

"One more time. Tonight. Come on!"

"Amy, please don't make me. I'm so scared I know I'll keep falling off my bike. Look, I can't even eat my macaroni and I love macaroni. Even in broad daylight I'm too scared to eat."

"Yeah, you're a wreck, all right. You wouldn't be any help, I can see that. Okay, I'll go alone. But there's something you've got to do for me."

"What?"

"You've got to be my cover."

"Your cover? What's that?"

"After school you come home with me. Ask my mother if I can stay overnight at your house."

"Well, sure, Amy. You've done that lots of times."

"Then tonight we'll go to bed early and I'll sneak out and—hey, Betty Lou! I'll bring you some Scotch!"

"Don't bother, I—"

"No bother. Who likes to drink alone?"

"Well, okay," Betty Lou said. "We still best friends?"

"Well, sure we are."

"Thanks. Hey, Amy, want my Jello?"

Amy laughed, picked up Betty Lou's dish of Jello and shook it. "Look, you eat it. You got something in common. It's as nervous as you are."

Betty Lou laughed too. A little.

Slowly, gradually, over the long hours that she lay in the cold, dark house, Nancy's mood of desolation and despair had turned to one of fierce determination. Her horror had given way to a furious indignation. Somehow, some way, she swore to herself, she was going to get out of this rotten mess. At any rate she was damned if she would be led like some unprotesting lamb to her slaughter.

She knew how high the odds against her were. For one thing she had, even in last night's flickering candlelight, recognized the Goldsmith living room, the furniture shrouded in dust sheets. She knew the house well, from when she was a child and had gone with her mother for tea with Mrs. Goldsmith. It was probably the most remote house on the island. Surely no one but its caretaker would have any reason to come near the place from early fall till summertime. So she could expect no help from anyone. She would have to deal with Andy herself.

And he was strong; enormously powerful physically, and he had a knife that was lethal. He had cunning, too—God, only she knew how much. He had killed Jim Barrow and *she* had stood trial for his murder. Oh, yes, he would get high marks for cunning. But he was basically a simple-minded man, and now his childish and insane fantasizing about her had taken him around the bend.

She had time on her side, too. She knew his motive

for kidnapping her hadn't been only money. His motive was vengeance, to punish her for "the dreadful thing she had done to him". But she felt sure he meant to let her live until he had collected the ransom. And the money couldn't possibly be delivered before tonight at the earliest. She began to hope that David would have difficulty raising a hundred thousand dollars quickly. That would buy her a little more time. But she knew he would get it. Dear David. Don't worry, David, darling, I'm going to get out of this and we're going to have one hell of a lot of wonderful years together.

She lay waiting for Andy to come back. Thinking, planning; hoping he would come soon.

The weather was threatening when Mickey Jamison started back to her office after a quick sandwich lunch at home. Crossing Fuller Street she saw Andy Fisher at the Davallion house on the corner. He was raking sodden leaves out from under a long hedge of forsythia. It was a difficult task, and he was so occupied that he wasn't aware of Mickey until she spoke.

"Hi, Andy," she said.

He turned to her, smiling his shy smile. "Oh, hello, Mrs. Jamison. How are you?"

"Okay. How are your rabbits?"

"Fine, thank you."

"How many you got now?"

"Six. But there'll be more in a few weeks."

"Congratulations." Mickey pointed to the pile of leaves he had raked. "Andy, why are you knocking yourself out doing that?"

"How do you mean, Mrs. Jamison?"

"Come spring and the forsythia grows, nobody can see those old leaves."

83

"I want them for my compost pile. I use a lot of compost in my gardens."

"Well, you're a great gardener, Andy. Keep doing what you're doing. So long, now."

"So long, Mrs. Jamison. Have a nice day."

Andy went back to his raking, smiling to himself. Everything was going just fine, just the way he had planned it. That Mrs. Jamison would never believe, no one in the world would ever believe that it was Andy Fisher who had kidnapped Nancy Ryan. Just like nobody had ever thought of him when the boat her mother and father had been sailing had caught fire and sunk. Or when he had killed her husband and made everyone think she'd done it. It wasn't his fault that she didn't spend the rest of her life in prison, as he had planned. It was the jury's fault when they let her off. That day had been the bitterest, the most frustrating day of Andy Fisher's life.

His scheme had been so clever, so inventive, that he had marveled at himself. He didn't know he could be so clever. And complicated as his plan had been, he had pulled it off without a single hitch. There had been no doubt in anyone's mind that Nancy's story was all lies and that she had killed Jim Barrow. If it hadn't been brought out at the trial that she was a battered wife, a fact as flabbergasting to him as to everyone else on the island, they would have found her guilty all right.

But it hadn't happened that way; she had got off scotfree, and after the trial she hadn't come back to the Vineyard, not even to get her clothes. He heard people say she wouldn't ever come back, not after what she had suffered here, and with everyone believing she had killed her husband. He'd thought maybe they were right, maybe she wouldn't come back. In that case he would have to go to her, wherever she was, so that he

84

could punish her for what she had done to him. And this time he wouldn't trust any judge or jury to do it. This time he would see to it himself.

And then, the month before last, in just one day he had heard two things that could solve his problem and change his whole life. He had been working at the Morton house on School Street that morning, he had mowed some grass and trimmed the hedges. Mrs. Morton had offered him a cup of coffee, and sat on the porch talking to him while he drank it. Very chatty old lady she was; would talk the ears off anyone who would listen to her. He was hardly listening, just nodding his head every once in a while, until he realized she was talking about Nancy Ryan. She was saying that Nancy was going to marry David Webster and wasn't that nice, him coming from such a fine old New England family, and wealthy, and wouldn't they make a handsome couple. Then she said they were coming back to the island. Coming back to the island to live!

That was the first thing he heard.

The second thing he heard was late that afternoon. He was in Falmouth at the nursery there, getting some shrubs for foundation planting at the Styles house. Jerry Maloney, one of the three gardeners who worked in the greenhouses, had waited on him. It was Jerry who told him that, come next year, Mr. Costello was going to retire. And when he did he would sell the nursery. Jerry said he would probably get close to a hundred thousand dollars for it.

Those were the two things that Andy heard, within the space of a few hours. Nancy Ryan was going to marry a very rich man. And the Costello Nursery in Falmouth was going to be for sale.

Andy had been buying his trees and shrubs, his potted plants and flats of seedlings, his seed and fertilizer and everything else he needed for his gardens at Costello's for as long as he had been gardening. Mr. Costello gave him a special discount that made the ferry trip to the Cape worth while. The nursery was the most beautiful place he had ever seen. There two long sleek greenhouses, whose thousands of small panes glittered like mirrors in the sunlight. Tables stretched along the walls and down the center, filled with trays of small blossoming flowers. Big baskets of rattan and macramé, trailing lantana and fuchsias and begonias, hung from the rafters. Outside there was a section where every kind of shrubbery and flowering tree and bush was stored, their roots enclosed neatly in burlap bags. And there was a shop where fresh cut flowers were for sale, with a giant glass-doored refrigerator, always filled with carnations and Shasta daisies and long-stemmed roses. Andy loved that place, loved everything about it. And now it was going to be for sale.

The idea hit him so suddenly, so vividly, that it left him staggered. Nancy was going to marry David Webster. They were coming back to the island. *Kidnap, ransom, kill, Costello Nursery*—the words whirled in his mind. He was going to punish Nancy as he had always known he would some day. But before he punished her, he would get the ransom from David to buy the Costello Nursery.

And then, oh, how his life was going to change! He wouldn't be Andy the gardener any longer. He would be Mr. Andy Fisher, the owner of the Andrew Fisher Nursery in Falmouth. Everybody would treat him the way they treated Mr. Costello—respectfully. Even though he was a foreigner with a funny way of talking, people were polite to him. The customers called him Mr. Costello, and they listened politely when he told them how to grow their flowers, and they thanked him and shook his hand. Oh, Mr. Costello was a somebody, all right.

And now Andy would be a somebody, too. He would take charge and give orders and people would listen to him and thank him for his advice. And then, if ever he found another girl he wanted to come and live with him, the way he had once wanted Nancy, she wouldn't lie to him and then betray him, the way Nancy had. It was because he was a nobody that Nancy and her parents had treated him so badly. But now he was going to be a somebody, with his own big greenhouses, and no one would ever treat him badly again.

CHAPTER ELEVEN

*T*HE CLOUDS WERE so heavy, the morning so dark and threatening, that David could barely make out the towns below him as the plane from Boston approached Cape Cod. But somewhere down there, on the Cape or near it, Nancy was being held prisoner.

David's father had been waiting for him at the bank in Boston, and the money had been turned over in a matter of minutes. Now the ransom, one hundred thousand dollars in fifties and hundreds, lay in a briefcase in his lap.

At the Vineyard airport David was the only one of the few passengers to approach the taxi stand, and he was grateful for that. If he had had to share a cab, to make conversation during the ten minute ride . . . no, he was in no mood to discuss the future of the Red Sox.

Mrs. MacWilliams was waiting for him in the front hall, her face haggard. "Thank heaven you're back," she said. "The police telephoned—"

"Jesus! They know?"

"No, it's not that. It's Nancy's car, they found it this morning out at Clam Bay."

"So that's where the bastard got her. What did you tell them?"

"That she'd gone for a walk there on the beach, and when she got back her car wouldn't start."

"And they bought that?"

"I'm sure they did. But, David, listen . . . they said there were tire tracks near her car, and footprints. They have to be the kidnapper's, don't they?"

"They could be, yes."

"Mightn't the police be able to identify the car by those tracks?"

"There's a chance," David said. "Of course there's a chance."

"Oh, David, I think you should call them! If there's a chance."

"He told Nancy that if I called the police. . . ."

"I know. But even if you don't go to them, and you pay the ransom, he may still . . . not let her go. Listen, David! It was Jimmy Corto who phoned, he's on the police force here now, and the two of you are old friends. Couldn't you trust him, couldn't you tell him?"

"Tell him unofficially?" David asked her. "Ask him to keep the kidnapping to himself?"

"That's it. Ask him to check those tire tracks on his own, as a favor to you. And the kidnapper would never know that—"

"All right," David said, "I'll do it."

Quickly, as if he were afraid he might change his mind, David reached for the phone and dialed the police number. It was answered at once.

"Officer Potter here," a policeman said.

"Is Jimmy Corto around?" David asked. "Could I speak to him?"

"Right here," Potter said. "Just a second."

In a moment Police Officer Corto was on the phone.

89

"Hi, Jimmy," David said, his voice cheerful, friendly. "This is your old buddy, Dave Webster. I just heard you were back."

"Yeah, old buddy," Jimmy said. "Congratulations to you and Nancy. And how is Mrs. Webster this afternoon?"

"Mending, thanks."

"Good. It's been a long time, Dave."

"Yeah, and it just occurred to me that we ought to do something about that. Like right away. Can you sneak off duty long enough for us to have a beer?"

"No sneaking necessary," Jimmy said. "I want to see you in the line of duty. It's about Nancy's car. How about in fifteen minutes?"

"Great, you bet," Dave said. "I'll be there."

Suddenly Mrs. MacWilliams was tugging at his arm, with her other hand she pointed to the window. David didn't have to look out to know what she meant. He could hear the rain slashing against the house, a sudden, wild, teeming downpour. In a matter of minutes those footprints and tire tracks would be washed from the sand.

"Damn it, Jimmy," David said, "but I can't make it this afternoon. I forgot . . . I've got to wait for a phone call from New York."

"Your publisher?"

"Right, that's the guy."

"I've read both your books, Dave. Nice going. Well, so long. Let's get together soon."

"I'll call you," David said.

"Whenever you say, pal," Jimmy said and hung up, looking puzzled. Dave's call must have had something to do with Nancy's car. But, Jimmy wondered, what had made him change his mind so suddenly?

When he got to Vineyard Haven, Tony Marcos found he had twenty minutes to kill before the ferry on which he would work the afternoon shift was due. The wind was cold and gusty, and he stepped into the waiting room to get out of it and light a cigarette. The place was unusually quiet even for winter; a few foot passengers, their tickets already purchased, sat in the long row of bright colored chairs. There was only one person at the ticket counter, and he was not buying a ticket. He was Tony's friend and colleague, Fred Nelson, and he had trapped poor Margie Riley behind the counter.

". . . and there we are, Tony and me, kidding the hell out of old Andy Fisher," Fred was saying. "Pretending we don't have a booster, stuff like that. Oh, it was really rich, Margie." Tony, listening, shook his head in a mixture of amusement and despair. He knew he'd be hearing Fred retelling this story many times in the days to come.

"But a funny thing was," Fred was going on, "when we pushed his pickup off the boat I seen something move under the tarp in the back and I asked him what it was. Well, sir, old Andy he turned white as a sheet. He said it was rabbits, a pair of Belgians he'd bought over at Buzz Campbell's place. But you know I been thinking it over, and Andy wouldn't do a thing like that to his rabbits—tie their legs together and throw them under an old tarp. He'd put them in a cage or a crate. And anyhow, what's all the secrecy about? So I say to myself, what's he *really* got under that tarp, the sly old dog. . . ."

Tony had heard enough. He ground out his cigarette and went out of the waiting room. He walked around looking for somebody who would bet against the Patriots in their game next Sunday. That was a somebody difficult to find anywhere in New England, and the ferry had landed before he could place a bet.

A few minutes later the phone on Mickey Jamison's desk rang and she answered it. "Island Realty Company, Mickey Jamison speaking."

"Hello, Mrs. Jamison."

She recognized the Irish voice. "Oh, hello, Mr. O'Hara."

"Do you have time for one more question?"

Mickey said she did, and O'Hara asked his question.

"Oh, sure, I remember," Mickey said. "Like I told you, I only saw Nancy for a second as I drove past, but I can tell you what she was wearing."

"I'd appreciate that."

"A yellow coat, dark-colored slacks, black or brown. And a scarf on her head, dark, too. Does that help any?"

"Well . . . but thanks anyway."

"Thanks for nothing, huh? Sorry, Mr. O'Hara."

"I've got to go back to work," Andy told her. "Is there anything else you want?"

"No," Nancy said.

"I can make you another sandwich," he said.

"No," she said quietly. Inside she was screaming at him to go, to get the hell out, to leave her alone so that she could make her escape. For the moment he was out of the house that was what she was going to do. She was going to set herself free.

"I have to tie you up again," he said.

"I know," she said, and she had to close her eyes before he could see the exultation and triumph in them.

It had happened, the miracle she had been praying for had happened!

Half an hour ago when Andy had returned, she had been listening to the rain beat ferociously on the roof and lash against the windows, the angry surf pound against the shore. He had opened the drapes on one window, facing the sea. Only a thin gray light drizzled through the rain-streaked panes. He had hung his rain gear over the newel post in the hallway.

He offered to let her use the bathroom, and she hadn't refused. He had undone her bonds and let her make her way on numbed and trembling legs, with him right behind her, to a downstairs back bedroom that had belonged to Tessie, the Goldsmith's long-time cook. He had even given her the stub off a sputtering candle to take into the dark bathroom.

She had known there would be no key in the door, no way to barricade herself inside, he would have made certain of that, and there was of course no window to escape through. Still, there was a medicine chest above the sink, and in it might be a bottle that she could break, or a nail file, or something she could use as a cutting tool. Please, Tessie, she prayed as she eased open the cabinet door and held the flickering candle up to light the shelves, please, Tessie, please have left something I can use.

Tessie had done better than she dared hope. Tessie had left a razor blade. It was old and slightly rusty, but it was a razor blade. Her fingers shook as she picked it up, wrapped it in her handkerchief and slid it into a back pocket of her jeans.

She hadn't refused, either, when he offered her food. He had given her bologna sandwiches and cupcakes and milk, and let her eat them sitting at the kitchen table. She was weak with hunger and she ate ravenously. She would need all the strength she could muster to escape.

Back in the living room, he was tying her up again. First the black electrical tape slapped around her wrists, to bind her hands behind her back; then he secured her ankles the same way. Finally a rope laced her securely to a straight chair. While he was winding the rope she inched her taped hands a bit to the right nearer the pocket that held the razor blade. He hadn't noticed. She thanked God for the darkness of the room, for surely Andy would otherwise have seen her excitement, the elation she couldn't conceal.

She heard him moving about the house, up the stairs, then back down. At last his footsteps sounded in the hall, the front door opened and creaked closed, and from the carriage house across the lawn she heard the pickup's motor starting and the wheels slosh through puddles and gravel left wet by the now dwindling rain. She made herself wait until there was utter silence before she even tried to reach the razor blade.

She started twisting her bound hands back and forth under the rope, straining against it. She felt it slacken a bit, but not enough; not nearly enough. Her hands had still not reached the pocket of her jeans. Dear God, was she going to make it?

Yes, she *was* going to make it! The razor blade had been heaven-sent and she wasn't going to let it go by. Ignoring the rope that rubbed against her skin until she was bleeding, mindless of the pain, she squirmed her hands farther down, closer to the pocket. She felt the sweat streaming down her face, felt the rapid pounding of her heart, and then, hardly daring to believe it, her fingers closed on the steel blade. For a moment she sat motionless, weak, utterly sapped by her efforts, her head spinning.

After a minute, when her breathing had returned to something near normal and her head had cleared, she drew the blade out of her pocket. Gripping it with her thumbs and forefingers, she began sawing at the nearest coil of rope she could reach. Back and forth, back and forth, over and over and over again. Don't get careless, Nancy, she warned. Don't get frantic. Don't break the precious blade, or drop it. You could still be sitting here tied to this chair when Andy comes back, any chance of escape gone. Carefully, she went on sawing, the blade at last broke through, the rope split open and she tumbled out of the chair onto the floor. The blade was still clutched in her fingers.

Lying on the floor, she drew her legs up behind her and began to attack the tape binding her ankles. It was difficult to reach but it took less time to cut than the rope. Then, struggling to her feet, she was running as fast as she could on her numbed legs, through the living room and into the center hall. It didn't matter that her hands were bound, she was able to turn the knob of the big front door. Then she was standing outside, almost delirious with the miracle of her escape.

She leaned against the railing of the veranda for a second to catch her breath and calm herself, and was surprised to see that it was not yet night. The sky was heavy, and a thin fog was rolling in from the bay, but it was still daylight. Those hours she thought she had spent struggling against her bonds must have, in reality, been only minutes.

She had just gone down the steps to the driveway when she heard the rumble of the pickup coming back. She looked wildly around. To the right and left the Goldsmith winter-brown lawn stretched out to stands of stunted trees; in the rear stood the carriage house. If

95

Andy should come back, shelter there was too far for her to reach before he would be upon her. She turned and started racing toward the back of the house and, passing the side of the veranda she saw what might be her salvation. Here, against the porch, was a foundation planting, a hedge of thick evergreens. She hurled herself at it, wriggled through, and crouched in its shadows. The branches had just sprung back into place when the truck stopped in the driveway. She heard Andy's outraged bellow, and knew he had seen the open door. His footsteps pounded up the steps to the veranda above her, then into the house, where they stopped dead. He had seen the empty chair, the severed rope. Then he was out of the house again, striding the length of the veranda, muttering inarticulate curses. He came down the steps and passed so close to her she could have reached out and touched him. His voice grew faint and distant and she thought he must have gone to search the beach. Now, she thought, if only by one more miracle night would suddenly fall, she could escape him in the darkness.

But he was coming back. She saw his legs pass her again, and then by a miracle even better than early darkness, Andy was starting his truck, was driving down the driveway through the woods, and in a minute was gone. She lay there in the mud and wet pine needles, shivering with the icy dampness, her arms sore and bleeding, wrists bound, body aching, and thought that she had never felt so good. She slithered her way through the hedge and got to her feet.

The beach, she thought, would be her escape route. It would be the shortest way to help, and the safest. Andy would surely be searching the woods between the house and the road.

Before she even reached the steps down to the beach his hands clamped down on her shoulders. He jerked her around to face him.

"You played a trick on Andy, didn't you?" he said. "But Andy played a better trick on you. You thought I was gone."

She rammed her knee into his stomach. She heard him grunt, and then his open hand slammed across her cheek, rocking her head with the force of his blow. Blinded by pain, groggy, she slid to the ground.

He lifted her in his arms like a rag doll and carried her back into the house.

CHAPTER TWELVE

*H*IS THEORY WAS a bust. O'Hara's legs were hurting again, even now, sitting in his car, even when stepping ever so lightly on the gas, ever so gently braking. He wasn't sure but he thought his right arm wasn't feeling well. Certainly his brain was ailing. After four days on this case he still had nothing. Zero. Worse than that. He was not only failing to prove Nancy Webster's innocence, he was proving her guilt.

Hello, retirement, you sonovabitch.

Where, now that he needed it most, he mourned, holding an Irish wake for himself, was the luck of the Irish? Face it, though, he wasn't completely eligible for the luck of the Irish. His mother, God rest her soul, was Polish, and the Polish were a notably unlucky people. He supposed he took more after his mother than his father. His dear brave mother had been unlucky enough to marry a lucky Irishman, who had drunk himself to death at an early age, leaving his Polish wife with three daughters and a son to raise. Come to think of it, where and when had the Irish been all that lucky?

Snap out of it, he told himself. For four days now he had thought about nothing but the case. It was time he gave himself a break. A five minute break. For five minutes he would think about something else. Pro football—the Patriots . . . pro basketball—the Celtics . . . Ethel Winston. How about inviting her out for dinner? Oh, forget it, she would probably say no. Nothing at all had been going right for him lately.

For a time, before he had talked to Mickey Jamison, he had been feeling pretty good. But that short phone call had ended that. Her answer to his question had been exactly the same as Ethel Winston's. "A dark scarf around her head," she had said, "dark slacks, a yellow coat. . . ." Wait a minute, now, he told himself. Maybe not *exactly* the same. Maybe he did have something after all.

As he was passing the garage on Main Street, he saw a small red sports car being towed in. It was a Mercedes, the one Nancy Webster drove. From what he could see of it, it didn't look damaged. He wondered briefly what had happened to it. But then, by that time, he was in town, and passing the Island Realty office. Through its broad window, filled with photographs of houses and water-front lots for sale, he could see Mickey Jamison at her desk. He parked in the first available space, walked back to the office, and went in.

By now Mickey was on the telephone. She smiled at O'Hara, waved him apologetically to a chair, and went on with her conversation.

". . . oh, sure, Mrs. McGrath, we've still got rentals for next summer," she was saying. "There's a couple over on Chappaquiddick you might like . . . yes, from June fifteenth through Labor Day . . . and then there's a big house right in town I know your kids would love . . . oh, and two or three others. Well, if you'd like to come over I'll be glad to show them all to you. Tomorrow? Okay, Mrs. McGrath, I'll meet the two o'clock ferry. ... fine. 'Bye, now."

She hung up and shook her head, smiling. "Oh, boy, but next summer's going to be a busy one. Only November, and the rentals are going like hot cakes. Well, what can I do for you, Mr. O'Hara?"

"Sorry to bother you again. Just one more question."

"Okay, shoot."

"It's still about what Nancy was wearing the night her husband was killed. Do you know if she owned a yellow coat *and* a yellow jacket?"

"No, just the one—the coat."

"You seem very positive."

"I am," Mickey said. "You see, Nancy didn't come back to the island after the trial. Ethel and I packed her clothes and sent them to her in New York. So I know exactly what she had. There was a beaver coat and a raincoat—a London Fog I think it was—a heavy green jacket, and the yellow coat I told you about. Ethel and I didn't think she'd ever want to see that again. I gave it to the thrift shop."

"Mrs. Winston described what Nancy was wearing as a jacket. You say a coat."

"I can explain that," Mickey said. "It was a car coat. You know? Longer than a jacket but shorter than an ordinary coat. Ethel and I were both right. Or both slightly wrong, by a few inches." The phone on the desk buzzed. "I'm sorry, Mr. O'Hara, I've—"

"Of course. Thanks."

O'Hara limped back to his car. Nothing. He was back to zero. His theory had turned out to be for the birds. But was he discouraged? Yes, he was. So discouraged that it did not even occur to him to get drunk, as it would have occured to any sensible Irishman, even a half-Polish sensible Irishman.

100

"Another piece of cake, Amy?"

"No, thanks—but it was some dinner!" Amy told Betty Lou's mother. "Don't tell my mother, Mrs. Weaver, but you're a better cook than she is."

"How nice of you to say so!" Marion Weaver said. "Betty Lou, have you ever told Amy's mother that she's a better cook than I am?"

"No, but I see my mistake," Betty Lou said. "I'll tell her the next time I see her."

"I hope you kids want to watch the same television show that I do," Betty Lou's father said.

"And what would that be?" Marion asked.

Evan Weaver looked at his watch. "In five minutes the President of the United States of America is going to solve the energy problem."

"Betty Lou and I don't have an energy problem. We ride bikes," Amy said. "We're going to bed now and listen to Elvis records, aren't we, Betty Lou?"

"Sure."

"After we do the dishes, of course," Amy said.

"I'll do the dishes," Marion said. "You two run along."

"Thanks. Good night, Mrs. Weaver," Amy said. "Some dinner!"

"Good night, Mom," Betty Lou said. "Good night, Daddy."

"Have fun, kids," Evan said.

"We will," Amy said. Then, upstairs in Betty Lou's bedroom with the door closed, she said, "At least I will."

"You will what?" Betty Lou said.

"Have fun. You sure you won't come with me?"

"Oh, yes!" Betty Lou said, "I'm positive."

In spite of the cold and her aching bones Nancy had fallen asleep. Andy's flashlight, focused on her face, had awakened her. She was in the small room on the second floor, where he had taken her after her attempted escape. Its only window was a little oval, cobweb covered, almost at ceiling height. By its pallid light she had seen she was in a storeroom. Piled along the walls were half a dozen crates and trunks, discarded furniture, an ancient sewing machine. Andy had dragged in a mattress from some other room. He had pushed her down on it, bound her again, tossed a blanket over her, and then without a word he left.

She knew it was now nighttime, for the tiny window near the ceiling was a black rectangle. The only light was Andy's flash. Once again he freed her hands and legs, and brought her downstairs to the living room, where a single candle sputtered. He gave her a sandwich and a glass of milk, and watched her while she ate. He waited until she had finished before he spoke.

"Now," he said, "it's time for you to make your phone call."

She closed her eyes. This was it, then, she thought. This was the end of the line. She would tell David how and where to deliver the ransom and he would do it. And after that, like her mother and father and Jim Barrow, she would be murdered.

"First," Andy said, "you will ask David if he has the money."

"He'll have the money," she said.

"You will tell him to put it in a briefcase, a plain black briefcase. And he should take it to the movie house in Edgartown. They start selling tickets at quarter to eight. You tell David he should be there first thing, he should be the first one to buy a ticket. You understand?"

"Yes."

102

"Then he should go to the men's room. There's a big trash basket there. He should put the money in the basket and cover it with paper towels. Then he should go in where the movie is and sit in the third row, right in the center. You got that, Nancy?"

She nodded.

"I'll be sitting there, watching him. You tell him. If he's brought in anybody who's a detective or a policeman or something like that, I'll know. And I guess he knows what will happen then."

"Yes, he knows."

"Tell him he should stay there until the picture is over. Then he can go—" He stopped suddenly and grinned at her. "That's all. That's all he has to know. And then, if everything goes right, when he gets home tomorrow night, you'll be there."

Her heart gave a jump. "Tomorrow? Not tonight? I thought you meant he should go tonight."

"You must have slept a long time," Andy said. "It's past nine o'clock. Too late tonight."

She felt as though sentenced to death, being led to the gallows, she had been pardoned. It wasn't true, of course. She wasn't free. She was still under sentence of death. But her execution had been postponed for twenty-four hours and in that time there would be another miracle. If it didn't happen by itself she would make it happen. She was going to escape.

Andy had taken the stub of a candle from the coffee table and carried it to the desk between two blacked-out windows. He pushed a chair up to the desk and pulled the telephone over to the edge.

"You call him now," he said.

She stood up and went to the desk. She reached for the phone but he snatched it from her.

"You told me to call—"

"But I'll do the dialing," Andy said, still smiling, proud of his shrewdness. "You maybe would dial 627-4343. And when the Edgartown police answer you tell *them* where and when to leave the money. Oh, no, *I* dial the number."

He raised the phone to his ear, and she watched his look of sly anticipation change to one of total disbelief, and then to indignant fury. He lowered the phone, staring at it as if it were some hateful monster. His rage exploded in a storm of hysteria.

"The misers!" he cried. "The greedy, stingy cheapskates! All the money they have. This great big house, their boats and their cars and all their hired help . . . and they turn off their telephone in the wintertime!"

Nancy watched him pace up and down the room, his hands clenched, muttering and cursing to himself, but never taking his eyes off her. Then, as suddenly, his mood changed again. His anger was gone, he was smiling.

"It's all right," he said. "I know where we'll go to telephone. It's safe enough and it's better this way. There's something I want to show you."

CHAPTER THIRTEEN

*B*ACK IN HIS ROOM at the Daggett House, after a good dinner that he couldn't bring himself to enjoy, Timothy O'Hara was dolefully going through his notebooks. He was trying to find some clue he had missed, some signal that would lead him up a new trail toward a solution of the Barrow case. So far he had drawn a blank. Now he was looking at the last page of his notes—a list of people to be interviewed. He had talked to all of them except one.

Old Mr. Danbury the notation read, with the name of Andy Fisher under it. Oh, yes, he remembered now why he had made that note, and why he hadn't acted upon it. He hadn't thought there was any chance of old Mr. Danbury being any help to him. But now it was clutch-at-a-straw time, O'Hara told himself. So start doing a little clutching.

He consulted the phone book and found that Danbury, Jared, and his street, town and telephone number were listed. He dialed the number. A man's voice answered.

"Mr. Jared Danbury?" O'Hara asked.

"Sorry, you've got the wrong number."

He hung up and thought, Jesus, O'Hara, you can't even get a phone number right any more. He looked it up again and dialed. This time a woman answered.

"May I speak with Jared Danbury, please?"

"He isn't here now," the woman said. "I'm his daughter. Can I help you?"

"I'd like to have a word with him. If I left my number—"

"No. He wouldn't call you. He never talks on the phone. Doesn't believe in it, thinks it's an instrument of the devil. But I'll tell you where you're sure to find him."

She told O'Hara that her father would be down at the town dock. He had been the Edgartown harbor master, she said, for forty-seven years, until his retirement nine years ago at the age of seventy-seven. But he still spent most of his time at the dock, making sure that everything was going smoothly there. Every night before he went to bed, weather fair or foul, he went to the dock for a final check.

O'Hara thanked her and hung up. So old Jared was retired, was he? Well, if old Jared couldn't give him a little help they would soon have something in common.

He went to the window. The upper deck of the dock was deserted. Thank God he wouldn't have to climb that long flight of stairs again. The Chappaquiddick ferry, on its winter schedule, was idle. He couldn't see all of the lower level of the dock, but what he could see of it was also deserted. Then an elderly man dressed in yellow oilskins strode into view. Jared Danbury? Probably. He looked like the man who ruled the dock. The harbor was his harbor, he was its master.

A few minutes later O'Hara walked onto the dock, and a spare but vigorous old man came hurrying to meet him, delighted to see him.

"Hello, there, young fella. I was just thinking—did I ever tell you about the time that—"

"You've never seen me before, sir."

"Never forget a face. About the time—"

"You're Jared Danbury?"

"Never claimed to be anyone else. About the time that singer fellow name of Sinatra tied up my whole dock with a yachtful of moving picture actresses? Yacht was so big I had to have the firemen down here fill its water tanks . . . ever tell you about that?"

"Yes, sir, just the other day," O'Hara said. "I understand, sir, that you were in the neighborhood of the Ryan house on the night Jim Barrow was murdered."

"Who told you that?" Jared demanded.

"Andy Fisher."

"He told you the truth! We met on Cooke Street near the Ryan house. He was over that way checking on the Fitzsimmons place. Checking the furnace or something, he told me. Then, I often had the Rockerfeller yacht here. I knew the Governor personally—"

"Yes, sir," O'Hara said. "Did you see anybody beside Andy that night?"

"Nope," Jared said, and took a deep breath.

O'Hara said quickly, "Andy says he saw someone. Leaving the Ryan house, he says. Do you think he did?"

"I don't know. Nobody believed him. Don't know why he'd lie about a thing like that. But then Andy, nice enough fella, except him and his rabbits. What's the point of caging up rabbits? They don't lay eggs. Only lay each other. Then there was the *Corsair*, J. P. Morgan's boat. Ever tell you about the time I had it here at my dock?"

"No, sir, go right ahead," O'Hara said. Jared Danbury was the last name on his list; he had nothing better to do. And maybe Jared could give him a lesson on retirement. "Tell me about J. P. Morgan and the *Corsair*, sir."

The blue truck moved down the driveway to the long, rutted lane that led to the Katama road, and then past fields and woods to the outskirts of the town. The streets at this hour were deserted. In only a few of the houses they passed were there any lights. They turned into a short, unpaved, dead-end road. At the end of it stood a single building, a small, lopsided house of weathered clapboard.

"This is my house," Andy told her proudly.

Taking her by her bound hands he led her across the yard to the door. It opened directly into a small, old-fashioned sitting room, dwarfed by a huge Franklin stove and oversized horsehair furniture. Behind it was a kitchen, larger than the parlor, with a coal range, an ancient icebox, a bare wooden table, a few chairs. She heard a soft crackling whisper, and saw a cage full of little furry creatures, ears tall, noses quivering, eyes staring unblinkingly in the overhead light. Andy's precious rabbits.

Andy opened the kitchen door and Nancy saw, immediately in front of her, a high stone wall. Built into it was a narrow door, fastened shut with a padlock. Andy unlocked it, pushed open the door, and led Nancy through.

"Look, Nancy," he said. "Look now."

He touched a switch and the place burst into a blaze of light. She saw that the stone wall, ivy-covered and far taller than she, surrounded what once had been an enormous garden.

In the center stood a fountain, a slender shaft that branched into clusters of copper cups. The water would cascade from one to another until it splashed finally into a small oval pool. In one corner was an arbor, the latticework fragile and gracefully wrought; in another a tiny gazebo. There were delicate bird baths placed here and there, and benches of mottled marble. And connecting them all were winding flagstone paths. She could see where there had once been formal flower beds, outlined with herbaceous borders, and where a rock garden had once encircled the pond. There were bowers of vines and shrubs—lilac and forsythia and honeysuckle. It must once have been, she thought, an enchanting place.

Now it was an ugly thing, a ghost garden, dead not of ordinary winter kill, but of negligence. Monstrous weeds had taken over, choking out the flowers, forcing their way between the flagstones, climbing up the stone walls. The copper fountain had turned a sleazy green, the little pool was filthy with dead leaves and twigs and slime. The slats of the arbor were broken, the bird baths and benches chipped. The shrubs and vines, untrimmed and uncared for, had gone wild. A magic garden turned into a tangled jungle.

"It was your garden, Nancy," he said. "I built it for you. I started it when you were still a little girl. Year after year I worked on it. I wanted it to be nice for you when you came here to live with me. And it was beautiful, Nancy. It was the most beautiful garden I ever made."

He moved closer to her, his voice was in her ear. She could feel his breath on her cheek.

"After your father and mother were dead," he said, "then I worked harder than ever, because I knew you would be coming to me soon. That's when I put in all these lights, and I worked late at night to get it ready for you. I thought you would be so happy you would laugh and clap your hands and hug me when you saw it. I thought—" He stopped, and when he spoke again his voice was bitter. "I never touched the garden again, not after you came back here with your husband. I hated the garden, I don't like to even look at it. In nice weather I let my rabbits play out here. That's all it's good for now, for my rabbits to play in."

Andy moved his hand, the bright lights were extinguished and the garden plunged into blackness. He and Nancy went back into the house, to a telephone in the kitchen.

"Now we'll make the call," he said, dialing the number. "Now you tell David what I told you to tell him."

David had closeted himself in the library, waiting for the call. He had sent Mrs. Mac to spend the evening with her friend Frieda Cass. He didn't want her to know any of the details of the ransom delivery—she was troubled enough by the knowledge of the kidnapping. When the phone rang at last he answered immediately. He told Nancy he had the money, then he listened carefully to his instructions. The Edgartown theatre at quarter of eight. . . the trash basket in the men's room. . . cover the briefcase with paper towels. . . sit in the middle of the third row. . . stay there until the picture has ended. . . .

"Have you got all that, David?"

"Yes, I've got it."

Then she raised her voice sharply and said, "You couldn't hear me, at the end? And now do you?"

"I heard you, Nancy—"

She interrupted him, her voice still raised. "I said wait until the end of the picture—stay in the middle of the third row until the picture is over . . . and now do you hear me? And now do you?"

"Yes. Yes, Nancy."

"That's it then, darling. Until tomorrow night—"

The connection was broken. He put the phone down. He knew what he was to do, he had heard the instructions clearly the first time. And Nancy knew he had. But still she had repeated the message. She was trying to tell him something, saying again that he was to wait until the picture had ended, to sit in the middle of the third row. And asking him could he hear her now.

She was trying to tell him something all right, but what in hell could it be?

Amy Lambert was no longer giving her undivided attention to Elvis Presley. She smiled as she remembered a conversation she had had last August with Sally Greer, aged thirteen, of Philadelphia. Last summer was the first that the Greer family had spent on the island. Sally had said that she loved the Vineyard, but how could Amy live here all year round? What, for goodness sake, did Amy do in Edgartown in the wintertime?

Well, Amy thought, tonight she would have more fun and excitement and adventure in little old Edgartown than Sally would have all winter in Philadelphia, Pa. She was disappointed that Betty Lou refused to go with her, but going alone would be even more of an adventure. She could hardly wait to get started. She would have been on her way long ago, but there had been a foul-up of her plan.

After watching the President's speech, Betty Lou's father and mother had not come upstairs to bed, leaving the coast clear for Amy. Instead they had invited their neighbors, the Shaws, over for a little bridge. It turned out to be quite a lot of bridge. It was almost eleven o'clock when the Shaws went home.

As soon as the house had quieted down, Amy shook Betty Lou. She had decided to give her one more chance. Betty Lou awakened reluctantly.

"They've gone to bed," Amy said. "I'm going now."

"Okay," Betty Lou said. "What time is it?"

"Eleven o'clock. You can still come with me," Amy said. "I'll wait while you dress."

Betty Lou burrowed under the covers. "No, I don't want to go! I told you."

"Oh, all right," Amy said. "Go back to sleep, you little chicken."

She slipped down the stairs and out the kitchen door. Then she was on her bike, pedaling through the dark, silent village, and on to the road that led to the airport. She laughed aloud into the night wind. At last she was on her way. She turned into the long dirt driveway running through a pine wood that made the Barnhardt house such a cinch, almost too easy to be much fun.

She leaned her bike against a tree in the Barnhardt's back yard and climbed the steps to their back porch. Three weeks ago she and Betty Lou had had to break a pane of glass to unlock the kitchen window. Now all she would have to do was push it up and crawl through, taking with her their two schoolbags, which she would take out again filled with Scotch and gin and vodka, enough to last them for weeks and weeks of secret parties.

She put her hands on the window frame to raise it. It didn't budge. She tried to put her hand through the broken pane, but there was no broken pane. The window had been repaired and relocked. Well, it wasn't going to be all that easy after all. Listening for any enemy sounds, she found a small stone in the yard, went back, and gently broke the same window again. She opened it and climbed through.

The Barnhardts kept their liquor in a dining room closet. Last time it had taken her and Betty Lou ten minutes to find it. This time she went directly to it, flung open the door, flashed her light in and gaped at what she saw. Instead of bottles and bottles of liquor, there was nothing. The cupboard was bare! Some greedy thief, Amy thought indignantly, had gotten there before her. How could anyone be so inconsiderate as to steal *everything?* She wouldn't have taken everything. She would have left something for other kids to find.

She went into the living room and sat down to figure out what to do. More than ever she wished Betty Lou were with her, to talk things over, make plans. Should she write off tonight, name it zilch? Or should she try somewhere else? After all, there were lots more empty houses, and most of them were sure to have liquor in them.

She just couldn't decide. She sure wanted some booze. It had been over a week since she'd had a single drink. On the other hand this wasn't much fun, breaking into a house all by herself. Darn it all, she thought, why hadn't Betty Lou come with her?

CHAPTER FOURTEEN

*H*E HAD PUT Nancy back in the storage room and was about to drive his truck into the carriage house when he remembered his rabbits. His *rabbits!* In all the excitement of the past two days he had forgotten all about them. He hadn't fed them since early yesterday morning. Even seeing them in the house tonight when they had gone to make the phone call to David, he hadn't remembered. The poor things would be so hungry. Their water would be gone, too, and they would be thirsty. They wouldn't know what to think. He had always taken such good care of them, buying them nice fresh vegetables and giving them cool fresh water and cleaning out their cages every day. He had to get back to them, and quickly. Those rabbits were his best friends.

He turned the pickup around and started back to his house.

Mr. Henry Jacoby was in bed, reading Hemingway's *For Whom the Bell Tolls* for the fifth or sixth time. For the past half hour, each time he finished a page, he had glanced at his wife. She was getting ready for bed. When he had finished reading page 143 he caught her sitting at her dressing table, staring at a stocking she had just taken off. When he finished page 146 she was halfway into her nightgown, standing motionless before the cold fireplace, staring down into it. Henry closed his book. He knew what was on Dottie's mind.

"Dottie, will you please stop worrying about it!"

She didn't have to ask him what he was talking about. She knew. "I'm not exactly worried about it, dear. As you pointed out, Nancy was acquitted. So it can't be important to anyone."

"So forget it."

"But Henry, I'm puzzled. And you know I can't bear having any unsolved puzzles in the house."

"Well, don't make a career out of this one."

"First chance I get," Dottie said, "I'm going to the library and look up the story in the *Gazette* files. And I promise you not to think about it till then."

"That's a good girl. For that I'm going to name my greenhouse after you. The *Dottie I.*"

"Henry, isn't a greenhouse rather drastic? And expensive?"

"Not this one. I'm going to build it myself."

"Oh, dear, the way you throw yourself into things! Your own greenhouse. I suppose you'll practically live in it."

"You can bet on that."

"Well, you know you'll have to give up throwing stones. And you love to throw stones."

Henry laughed. "Good night," he said, snapping off his reading lamp.

"Good night," Dorothy said.

Nancy tested the tape at her wrists and ankles. Andy had done his work well this time. He had bound her even tighter than before; she sure as hell wasn't going to free herself this time. Now, she thought grimly, her only hope was the signal she had tried to send Dave over the telephone. Andy had cut the connection—she didn't know if Dave had understood. It was a wild, crazy message, and it would be a miracle if he was able to decode it.

She heard footsteps somewhere on the floor below and knew that Andy had come back. She hoped he wouldn't come into the storeroom. She couldn't bear the sight of his stupid, smirking face. The steps came closer, they were directly under her now, and she could hear that they were not Andy's way of walking.

Then she realized that she hadn't heard the pickup truck, or the creaking that the front door always made. And she knew it wasn't Andy Fisher moving about the house. It was someone else.

At the top of her lungs she screamed for help. And then the footsteps came upstairs and along the hallway, stopping outside the storeroom.

"Here I am!" she called. "In here! Help me!"

She heard the key click in the lock—knowing she was securely tied, Andy had left it on the outside of the door. The beam of a flashlight groped around the room, found the mattress, settled on Nancy's face.

"Nancy!" a young girl's voice said. "Oh, Nancy!"

"Who is it? Who are you?"

The beam tilted into the girl's frightened face. "It's me, Amy Lambert!"

"I've been kidnapped, Amy! Get a knife, scissors. In the kitchen. Hurry—"

They heard it then, both of them heard the sound of a truck as it passed the house on its way to the carriage house. Oh, dear God, Nancy thought, what would he do to the child if he found her her?

"Amy, run! Get out of here before—"

"Yes—I'll get the police!"

Amy turned off her flashlight, groped her way out of the storage room into the hall. There her outstretched hand found a bannister, and she felt along it to the top of the stairway. She had started down when below her the fanlight over the front door turned crimson, as a flashlight from the outside splattered the red glass. Amy retreated back up the steps into the hall before the front door opened. There were footsteps, and a beam of light in the hall, moving toward the back of the house, and then both disappeared.

Quickly, Amy slithered down the stairs to the window she had broken in a front room when she entered. She was through it in a second and out on the porch. She could see a flashlight moving around inside the house. She scrambled down to the ground.

Her bike was on the other side of the house, leaning right up against it. She didn't dare try to get it. She was even afraid to go out onto the lawn that surrounded the Goldsmith house—the kidnapper might see her from a window. She didn't know what he would do to her if he caught her. Maybe tie her up, like he had Nancy. . . .

She thought about how terrible Nancy had looked, how sick and scared, and she knew she had to take the chance, she had to get help for Nancy. Lying flat on her stomach she started squirming across the lawn toward the grove of dwarf oaks beyond it. Any moment she expected to hear a window fly open, an angry voice bellow at her to stop or he would shoot . . . or maybe he would come through the window after her, and his hurtful hands would lift her by her shoulders. . . . She sobbed in relief when she reached the shelter of the woods.

117

Now the kidnapper couldn't see or hear her from the house. She got to her feet and started to run. The branches of the little trees slapped at her face, brambles tore at her jeans, snagged at her ankles. But still she ran, as fast as she could, fighting her way through the underbrush, panting, until at last she reached the road.

And now, oh, how she wished she had her bike! With her bike she could pedal to the police station in maybe fifteen minutes. But without it. . . .

Suddenly, there were headlights behind her. Someone was coming down the road. Turning around to face it, she stood in its path and waved her arms wildly in the air.

The headlights stopped just short of her. She ran past them. "Oh, help me, please," she gasped. And then she saw the blue pickup and its driver, and knew it would be all right—he was a friend of hers. "Oh, thank goodness it's you. Listen, Andy, the most terrible thing. . . ."

CHAPTER FIFTEEN

O'HARA HAD NOTICED, the several times he had driven past the Ryan house, that only three houses in that block of Cooke Street seemed to be occupied this winter. There was Ethel Winston's house, next to the Ryan's, and another, diagonally across the street. The third one was farther down the block, but close enough to the Ryan place to make O'Hara think that talking to the owners might be of some help to him.

This morning he had found Mr. and Mrs. Knapp just finishing breakfast. Charles Knapp was one of Edgartown's most successful real estate brokers. His busiest time was, of course, the spring and summer; his slack time, the winter. His wife and he usually spent January and February in Florida. The year of the murder, however, they had splurged and taken a November to January rental at the Riverbend golf club in Tequesta, not far north of Palm Beach. So on that night that was fatal for Jim Barrow, they were far from the scene of the crime.

"But thank you," O'Hara said. "Thank you very much."

For nothing, O'Hara said to himself. So far that seemed to be all he had to thank people for. Nothing. And so far Nancy Webster had nothing to thank him for, either.

Henry Jacoby stood in his living room, looking out the window at a dreary, cloud-filled sky. It was Dorothy's morning to work as a volunteer at the hospital in Oak Bluffs. She wouldn't be home much before lunch time, and Henry Jacoby was lonely. Well, he thought, for thirty years Dottie had waited for him to come home from the office, now it was his turn to do a little waiting. Sometimes when she was made to wait unusually long, Dottie would have a little drink. Well, he could hardly have a drink so soon after breakfast. Or could he? No, he could not.

Still gazing out the window, he saw a man come out of the Knapp house down the street. As he came closer, walking slowly, Henry saw that his face was the proverbial map of Ireland, and Henry would have bet he was an ex-cop. Then the indisputably Irish ex-cop was turning in at the Jacoby house and knocking on the door. Almost immediately Henry learned that this ex-cop was indeed an Irishman named Timothy O'Hara. Surprisingly, however, he was not an ex-cop, but a journalist doing a story on the Barrow murder case.

"Have you lived here long?" O'Hara asked. "You have a big city look, maybe New York. Madison Avenue? Advertising, maybe?"

Henry laughed but did not mention that his visitor was a better judge of a man than he. He admitted to having once been on Madison Avenue, and said right now he needed some advice. Did O'Hara think it was too early in the day for a drink? O'Hara carefully considered Henry's question, and said it depended on the size of the drink. He suggested it not be a big drink, just a medium drink, but not too medium. In no time at all, sipping their not-too-medium drinks, they got down to business.

"We bought this house five years ago," Henry said, answering a question of O'Hara's "but this is our first winter here."

"So obviously you can't help me," O'Hara said. "You weren't here when Jim Barrow was murdered."

"Well," Henry said, "I was and I wasn't."

"Did I hear you right? You were and you weren't?"

"I can see where that might need a little explanation. We were still living in New York, Dottie and I. I hadn't yet retired." Henry didn't notice that O'Hara winced at that word, and he went on. "I was scheduled to make a speech. Some advertising thing, big deal. Actually, it did seem important to me at the time. I was having trouble writing it, couldn't get it moving. Dottie suggested I come up here, alone, and work on it. No New York distractions. It seemed like a good idea to me. The meeting was to be in Boston. Perfect solitude for me here, convenient, made good sense."

"You have a wife who makes very good sense," O'Hara said. "Not always the case. You're lucky."

"Dottie makes good sense, a good apple pie, and a delicious dry Martini. And she's a beautiful girl. Well, I drove up and came over on the last ferry. Didn't see anyone I knew. Drove over here, got the car in the garage and myself into the house without anyone knowing I was here. Decided to keep it that way. Absolute solitude. No distractions, no excuses. I'd write a hell of a speech. Before I turned on any lights I pulled down all the shades, and I slept and worked in the downstairs bedroom, off the kitchen. We kept the heat on during the winter, thermostat set at fifty—the energy crisis

121

wasn't as bad as it is now—it was comfortable. Dottie had the pantry well stocked with canned stuff, so I had enough to eat. I never stuck my nose out of this house for two solid days and nights."

"You weren't even aware of the murder then?" O'Hara wanted to know.

"Yes, I was aware of it. It was the second day I'd spent here, the night of the second day. I was still working on my speech, just finishing it up. It was about ten o'clock when I heard the commotion. Police sirens on this street, stopping close by. Quite a commotion. Another police car stopping in front of the Ryan house, more cops going in. Doc Rankin arriving. And after a while an ambulance, and a body carried out of the house."

"You still didn't know what happened?"

"Oh, yes. Radio—local station. I heard that Jim Barrow had been murdered. They thought at the time it was the work of a burglar. Well, I hadn't heard or seen one damn thing until the first police car arrived, there wasn't anything I could tell anybody. There didn't seem to be any point in my getting involved. And so I didn't."

"You didn't have any particular feeling about Nancy and Jim Barrow?"

"We hardly knew them. Dorothy and I didn't come up that year until early July—the Fourth of July weekend, as a matter of fact. The Barrows were here—they'd come about a month earlier, I think. And we closed the house and went back to New York right after Labor Day. So it was only for those two months that we were neighbors. Said hello when we passed them, waved from the car. Of course they were kids, we wouldn't have become great friends in any case, but they were having their troubles that summer. Nobody saw very much of them."

"Yes, I see."

"At any rate, Mr. O'Hara, that's what I mean when I said I was here and I wasn't. And I'm afraid I can't be of any help to you."

"I'm afraid you're right, Mr. Jacoby," O'Hara said, and sighed. "How did the speech turn out?"

"Frankly, I was a sensation."

"Thanks to your wife," O'Hara said.

"Thanks to my wife," Henry said. "If you're in the neighborhood again, drop in for one of her dry Martinis and some apple pie."

"My favorite combination," O'Hara said. "And you make one hell of a medium drink." He put on his coat and left.

At approximately ten o'clock Saturday morning, Evan Weaver suggested to his wife that they take their binoculars and go watch some birds at Felix Neck. Although Marion was an avid bird watcher, she refused. She said she wanted to stick around and see that Betty Lou and Amy ate a healthful breakfast, not just Cokes and Fritos. She urged him to go alone or, better still, invite Dottie Jacoby to go with him.

Evan decided against that. In a small New England village going bird watching with another man's wife was not the thing to do. In small New England villages, in the dullness of winter, people talked. About each other. Whose husband was seen bird watching with whose wife on Felix Neck last Saturday? Evan went to Felix Neck alone.

Marion went to the stairs and listened. No music, no girlish giggling. Thirty minutes later she listened again. Still all was quiet. She decided the girls had slept long enough—besides, she wanted to get breakfast out of the way.

"Betty Lou!" she called. "Amy!"

Betty Lou struggled out of a deep sleep. "Hey, Amy," she said, and turned over to find that Amy wasn't there. She was instantly awake. She ran to the bathroom and found it empty. She saw that Amy's schoolbag and her clothes were gone. Looking out the window she could see her own bike leaning against the porch. Amy's bike was gone.

Marion opened the door. "Good morning, you sleepy heads," she said, smiling. Then she said, "Where's Amy?"

"She had to go home," Betty Lou said.

"For heaven's sake! Why?"

"I don't know. I don't remember why."

"You girls didn't have a quarrel, did you?"

"No. Listen, Mom, I am really starving."

"Okay. Breakfast on the table in ten minutes." Marion started out, then turned back. "I didn't hear anything. What time did Amy go?"

"Oh, early," Betty Lou said. "Before anyone was up. Will you make scrambled eggs with bacon?"

"All right," Marion said, and went down the stairs.

Betty Lou sighed mightily. She certainly hoped that what she had told her mother would turn out to be true, that Amy had gotten up early and gone home. Or maybe she had found so much liquor at the Barnhardt house that she wanted to get it home and stashed away before her parents were awake. Yes, that must be it. That must be what had happened.

The island ferry, bound for the mainland now, slid out of its berth and picked up speed. On its upper deck Dave checked his watch. The boat had left almost on schedule; in forty minutes it would be docking in

Woods Hole. And then, for the first time since Nancy's phone call two nights before, he would be doing something positive, thank God. He would be tracing Nancy and her kidnapper. It was a long shot, a slim chance, but he was high with hope. He had found out the number of the phone in Pocasset from which Nancy had made the call.

He looked again at his watch; thirty-five minutes now. And then he heard his name being called, and turned to see the last person in the world he wanted to see; his old friend and childhood buddy Jim Corto. There was no escape. He made his grin as broad as Jimmy's, his handshake as cordial.

"Dave!" Jimmy was saying. "How are you, old chum? And is Nancy all better?"

"Almost better, but still housebound. Where are you off to, Jimmy, all dressed up like a cop?"

"Going over to Falmouth to collect a robbery suspect we're interested in. Dave, I'll buy you a beer, and me a Coke, on account of I'm all dressed up like a cop. Okay?"

"Sure," Dave said, "you bet."

Seated at a table in the lunchroom with their drinks before them, Jimmy said, smiling, "Hey, Dave, you're looking pretty good. Much better than I thought you would."

"And you're fairly well preserved, too, old pal. Oh, incidentally, thanks for writing me. When was it—five, six years ago you said you were off to see the world and seek your fortune. I said good luck, write me, keep in touch."

"And what did I say, Dave?"

"You said you would, but you lied in your teeth. I never heard a word. What happened? Tell me all about yourself. If you insist."

"Well, I didn't see much of the world—or find my fortune. I got to California, and then Easton, Pennsylvania, where I ended up being a cop. This summer my folks wrote me there was an opening on the Edgartown force, so here I am."

"Easton's loss is also Edgartown's loss," David said. "Welcome home, Jim."

"Welcome to you and Nancy, too. Hey, about Nancy's car—"

"No problem. The garage towed it in."

"Mrs. Mac tell you that the rotor was missing?"

"No, she didn't, but the garage will take care of it. Say, Jimmy, did you get to San Francisco?"

"Didn't get north of Fresno. Dave, about that rotor. It could have been kids, malicious mischief, but then—"

"Sure, that's it. Jimmy, whatever happened to—"

"Dave, listen. It may not have been kids. There are some people on the island who . . . well, who aren't exactly Nancy's friends. One of them might have immobilized her car to harass her. And if that's happening I'm not—excuse the expression, but I'm not doing my duty."

"No," David said, "that's not happening, Jimmy."

"No one's been bothering her?"

"No one."

"You leveling with me? I know it's tough to talk about it."

"Let's say there's no reason to talk about it. It's all over and done with, everything's okay."

"So okay, Dave, now I'll let you change the subject, and why don't you?"

"I thought you'd never ask. Is old Mr. Danbury still alive and kicking?"

"If you stopped writing books for a few minutes and walked down to the town dock you'd *see* him still living and kicking."

126

"He can't still be harbor master! He must be ninety!"

"Almost. No, he isn't harbor master any more but he won't admit it. Practically lives on the dock. Hey, Dave, remember his granddaughter?"

"Ginger? Our Ginger! My God, was she ever stacked!"

"So stacked," Jimmy said enthusiastically, "it was frightening."

"Whatever happened to our Ginger?"

"She married a guy that plays defense for the Pittsburgh Steelers."

"That's good," David said. "So I guess she doesn't frighten him."

"She sure had a crush on me," Jimmy said. "What I missed!"

"Wait a minute," Dave said. "She had a crush on you?"

"Sure, she was always hanging around me."

"Wait a *minute*," Dave said. "Let's get this straight. Ginger was hanging around *me*, and you just happened to always tag along, you damn nuisance."

"It was me she loved," Jimmy said, grinning. "She kept telling me so."

"She couldn't have told you all that much," Dave said, "because she told me about every five minutes she was head over heels in love with me."

"What a two-faced dame," Jimmy said.

"Just goes to show," David said, "you never can trust a thirteen-year-old woman."

CHAPTER SIXTEEN

*F*OR A TIME NOW, ever since a turbid morning light had crawled through the high oval window, they had heard him moving about the house, pacing the floors, going up and down the stairs. Although the light in their room had not changed, it was still a sunless murky gray, Nancy knew that hours must have gone by; she guessed it was around midmorning. Finally they heard the big front door open and shut, the sound of his footsteps on the porch and then on the graveled drive.

"Nancy," Amy whispered, "is he going?"

"I think so," Nancy said. "Listen for his truck."

In a moment they heard the engine cough and turn over, and the sound of its crescendo as it came past the house and gradually faded away. They were lying side by side; Amy's hands and feet were bound as securely, and as painfully, as Nancy's were. All night long, ever since Andy had tied her up and left her on the mattress beside Nancy, she had been struggling to free herself, and that brought only more pain, more frustration. Now she lay quiet, exhausted, listening again, still not believing what was happening to her. She told herself she was dreaming, she would soon wake up and find it was Betty Lou beside her, not Nancy Webster.

"He's gone," Nancy said to her.

"But he'll be back?"

"Oh, yes," Nancy said, "he'll be back."

"That rotten old bastard, Andy Fisher," Amy said furiously. "Always acting like he was such a nice guy! Him and his darling rabbits! And then going around kidnapping people! Oh, Nancy, I—I'm *scared*!"

"No, you're not. I don't believe it."

"I am, I really am!"

"Don't forget, Amy, I'm your old baby sitter. I know you've never been afraid of anything in all your life. You were always fearless."

"Was I? Honestly?"

"Fearless," Nancy said, "and tough. You never cried when you fell down. You climbed the highest trees, you swam farther out than any of the other kids. You could do anything."

"Gee, I was pretty good, wasn't I, Nancy?"

"Except when you were pretty bad."

"What did I ever do bad?"

"Remember when you sneaked into the five-and-ten and set all the mousetraps?"

"Yeah, I remember that," Amy said, smiling. "That was fun."

"And the time you set all the alarm clocks in the hardware store?"

"I don't remember that. How old was I?"

"About six or seven."

"Hey, I was pretty smart for a kid my age, wasn't I? And I was never scared." She grinned shakily. "Well, my streak is over now. Tell me again, Nancy. He isn't going to hurt us, is he? Keep telling me he isn't."

"Of course he isn't," Nancy said firmly, knowing that

if Andy Fisher killed her, he would kill Amy, too. "No," she said again, "of course he wouldn't hurt us."

"All he wants is the money, isn't it?"

"Yes, and that's all arranged. David will give it to him tonight."

"At eight o'clock, you said."

"Eight o'clock," Nancy said. "At the theatre."

"So we've got only today to wait."

"Yes," Nancy said, "that's all."

"And that's not so bad, is it? Not all that bad."

"Not at all that bad," Nancy said.

But it was bad, Amy thought, and she was still scared. She wished she could believe Nancy that nothing could go wrong. Things could go wrong. People who got kidnapped did sometimes get hurt. Sometimes worse than that. But she was grateful to Nancy. She wished she could think of something to say to make her think she wasn't scared. Something funny, for instance. But it was pretty hard to think of anything funny when you were scared.

"Hey, Nancy, please tell me some more about what a brave kid I am."

"Okay, remember the time you. . . ."

Andy was making the rounds of his houses, carefully checking, as he always did, the locks on the doors, the windows, rotating the lights to discourage burglars, making sure that no leaks had developed from the drenching rain the afternoon before. There was a lot to do, and he had been late getting started. It had been hard for him this morning to get moving, to leave the Goldsmith house and go about his chores. That thing the night before, the Lambert girl coming, had unnerved him.

It had just been plain luck that he had noticed the bicycle outside the house. That had alerted him. In a matter of minutes he had searched the house, seconds after that he was back in his truck. It was easy to catch up to the girl and bring her back; she had thought they were going there to rescue her friend, Nancy.

As he left the Jenner house on Atwood Circle, he locked the front door, made certain it was secure, then walked around the place, checking it on all sides. In the back yard he saw that the little duck pond had overflowed its banks, the first time that had ever happened. The water was lapping right up against the flagstone terrace. He hadn't realized how hard the rain yesterday had been. He wondered suddenly if, after all his preparation, his supply of gasoline was big enough. God, he had to have enough gasoline. Everything depended on that.

He got in his truck, drove out of town to his house, loaded his leaf blower and an empty five-gallon gasoline can onto the pickup and started back to town.

Andy decided he had better not go to the Texaco station; he had been there already this week. Twice, in fact, filling his cans with gas. He drove instead to the Mobil place. As Bobby Fallon filled the gas can, he said, "You're not still mowing lawns, are you, Andy?"

"No," Andy said, smiling. That was the question he wanted to be asked. He jerked a thumb at the machine in the back of his truck. "I got some leaves to blow."

"All the rain we had yesterday," Bobby said, "those leaves will be too matted down."

"Not for my blower," Andy said. "It can handle them."

Now for sure he would have enough gasoline, more than enough, for what he had to do tonight at the Goldsmith house, right after he had collected the ransom.

Timothy O'Hara was making sure that he had not forgotten anything. He checked the closet, the chest of drawers, the bathroom. He had not forgotten anything. Congratulating himself for at last doing something right in Edgartown, he closed his suitcase, went downstairs, and paid his bill. He saw that he had plenty of time to catch the noon ferry.

When he had phoned his office to make his progress report, or rather his lack-of-progress report, Cap Andrews had ordered him to throw in the towel and get the hell back to Boston. He had called Nancy Webster then to tell her he had been taken off the case. Her husband had answered, told him that she was ill, unable to come to the phone. O'Hara was surprised that he felt such deep concern for her. Such a charming girl, such a pretty, pleasant young woman. He knew that his angry disappointment in himself for handling the case so ineptly was as much because of failing Nancy as it was because he failed himself. And fail he certainly had.

Well, the end would be painful, but it would be quick. He would be retired, probably on his next payday. With his pension and his social security he could afford to see the Red Sox a couple times a week, in the fall some Patriot games, then the Bruins for hockey and the Celtics for basketball. And then there was television. That didn't sound so bad. And he had his memories of when he had been one of the best private eyes in Boston. It didn't sound so bad at all—the hell it didn't. It sounded lousy.

On the ferry he bought himself a beer and found an empty table in the corner of the lunchroom. In the middle of his second beer he heard a cheerful, familiar voice sing out, "Why, hello there, Mr. Timothy O'Hara! May I join you?"

He looked up from his glass to see Ethel Winston

132

coming toward him, looking better than ever. Her figure in smart city clothes—a slim tweed suit with a beaver collar and shiny black boots—was absolutely smashing. Her eyes, still the bluest he had ever seen, were sparkling. My God, he thought, this beautiful lady was glad to see him. Immediately he stopped feeling sorry for himself.

"Don't get up," she said as she slid into the bench across the table from him. "So your research is done. You're on your way home now to do the writing."

"Yes," he lied, and said quickly, "did anyone ever ask you if you were once a Miss America?"

"Lord bless the Irish!" she said. "I do love a bit of blarney now and then."

"All dressed up," he said, turning on a bit of a brogue. "Would you be meeting Burt Reynolds, or maybe Robert Redford on the other side?"

"Now you've gone too far," she said. "No such luck. I'm on my way to try to cheer up an aged aunt of mine in a depressing old folks' home in Falmouth. I'm taking her out for lunch."

"You'll cheer her up. The sight of you has already done that for me."

"You are an adorable man! Well, if I don't cheer my Aunt Clara up, I'm sure the yellow chrysanthemums I got for her will."

"No yellow chrysanthemums ever cheered me up."

"My aunt jumps for joy at the sight of yellow mums. It's her favorite flower. Not that it is any business of mine, but why do you need cheering up?"

For an instant O'Hara had an impulse to tell her the truth, perhaps to cry a little on her elegant shoulder. Instead, getting a grip on himself, he said, "I've been smitten by your island. I hate to leave it."

"But you live in Boston, don't you?"

"Right."

"Seventy miles away. No problem. And you're a writer, you can live wherever you wish. Why not live on the island? Many writers do. There, I've solved your problem, and you have just solved one of mine."

"Well, good for me. How have I solved a problem for you?"

"Your necktie. That is a splendid necktie. I am going to buy one like it for Henry Jacoby. The Jacobys are neighbors of mine. They bought the old Fitzsimmons house across the street from me. A darling couple."

"I've just met him," O'Hara said. "Say, isn't it time we were getting to our cars?"

"Yes, it is."

It turned out that O'Hara's car was on the same side of the ferry as Ethel's, so that he not only had the pleasure of escorting her to it but of seeing the chrysanthemums she was taking to her aunt, a huge flowering plant in a foil covered pot.

"But I thought," O'Hara said, "that your aunt's favorite flowers were yellow chrysanthemums."

"Yes," Ethel said.

"Those are yellow?"

"Aren't they?" Ethel asked.

"They are red, as in red, white and blue. And, Mrs. Winston, you are either color blind or you are out of your mind."

"Damn," Ethel said. "Tony promised to send me yellow mums. Aunt Clara hates red, anything red, she—"

"Mrs. Winston, this is important," O'Hara said. "You really *are* color blind?"

"Yes. And not the ordinary mistaking-red-for-green color blindness. I see everything in black and white. I've been color blind all my life, it isn't against the law—"

"But you told me," O'Hara said, "that on the night of

the murder you saw Nancy wearing a yellow jacket."

"Yes, I did. She was."

"If you can't tell a red flower from a yellow one—"

"How could I know Nancy was wearing a yellow jacket? Well, I didn't at the time, I didn't know what color it was. But after the trial Mickey Jamison and I packed Nancy's clothes to send to her in New York. Mickey pointed out a jacket and said it was the yellow thing she'd worn the night of the murder, and let's not send it. That's how I was able to tell you it was yellow. No one ever brought it up, no one ever asked me before. I don't see why it matters."

The line of cars in front of Ethel's began to move off the ferry. O'Hara said quickly, "Will you wait for me? Believe me, it's important."

"Yes, of course."

"By the ticket office, okay?"

"Okay," Ethel said.

It was five minutes later that O'Hara pulled his old Pontiac up beside Ethel's fairly new Volvo, got out of his car, and opened the door of the Volvo.

Ethel said, "Put the damn red mums on the back seat."

"Beautiful red mums," O'Hara said, putting the flowers on the back seat with loving care. "They just might be the key to proving Nancy didn't murder Jim Barrow."

"Oh, God, how wonderful that would be! And what a wonderful story it will be for you to write."

"Won't it though? Look, Mrs. Winston, Nancy says she was at the flower box for only a few seconds, getting a key. You testified she was there for at least three minutes, long enough to bury the gun. If she's telling the truth she's innocent, if you are she's guilty. Obviously one of you has to be wrong, or lying."

"I wish to heaven it was I, Mr. O'Hara. Please prove me wrong."

"I haven't known either of you very long," O'Hara said, "but long enough to make me decide neither of you was lying, or wrong. I thought maybe both of you were right."

"But how could that be?"

"I don't think it was Nancy you saw at the box. I think you saw the murderer, wearing one of Nancy's coats and a scarf, burying the gun."

"Oh, God," Ethel said. "Why didn't anyone ever consider that possibility?"

"Because everyone took for granted right from the beginning that Nancy was guilty."

"Mr. O'Hara, you must go to the police with this—"

"Not so fast. I haven't proved my point yet, not even to myself. But with your help I may be able to. You see, if the person Mickey saw was Nancy, and you saw the murderer, the two of you might have noticed something different about them."

"But if we both saw the same person?"

O'Hara shook his head. "Then we wouldn't have a chance of proving anything, would we? But I was working on the premise that you didn't see the same person. That's why I asked both of you what she was wearing. If your answers had been different, that would be the evidence I need. Unfortunately, you both said the same thing. Dark slacks, a scarf around her head, a yellow coat."

"No, not a coat," Ethel said. "I said a jacket."

"Yes, I caught that, and I talked to Mickey. She said she should have said a car coat, which is shorter than a regular coat, longer than a jacket."

"No," Ethel said, protesting, "the person I saw was wearing a short jacket. That's it! It was the murderer I

136

saw! Oh, Mr. O'Hara, you should have been a detective, not a writer!"

"Funny you should say that," O'Hara said, smiling.

"Why? Funny how?"

What was it about Ethel Winston, O'Hara wondered, that made him want to tell her about himself? Maybe it wasn't Ethel, maybe it was his own ego. He had just proved to himself that he was a detective, maybe he wanted to boast about it a little. One thing was sure, though; he wanted to boast about it to Ethel Winston. Like a kid on a bike. Hey, look, Ethel, no hands!

He told her he was a detective, employed by Nancy Webster to try to prove her innocence in the Barrow murder.

"But you said you were leaving the island because your research—actually your investigation—was completed. Obviously it isn't. I'm confused."

"I had given up," O'Hara admitted. "A total dead-end. Nancy Webster had to be guilty. But then, God bless you, Madam, you turned out to be color blind."

"Glad I could be of service," she said, laughing. Then, seriously, she said, "If there's anything I can do to help you. . . ."

"There's something that still bothers me. When you were packing Nancy's clothes and Mickey showed you the coat she said Nancy had been wearing, why did you agree with her?"

Ethel frowned, trying to remember. "If she had held it up, then I would have realized it wasn't the coat I had seen. But it was folded up on the bed. I just glanced at it and assumed it was. Oh, Mr. O'Hara, you'll go back to the island, won't you? You'll go to the police?"

"After a little more checking, yes."

She looked at her watch. "The ferry will be going back in fifteen minutes."

"I'll be on it," O'Hara said, smiling. "I'll check in at the Daggett House and I won't leave the island again, so help me, Mrs. Winston, until we get to the bottom of this."

"And I'll be coming back on the three forty-five," Ethel said. "I'll be home by five at the latest. Will you phone me? Keep me posted?"

"I'll do better than that. I will be at your house to report at five o'clock promptly, I promise. Good-bye, Mrs. Winston. Thank you, and God bless."

"The same to you, Mr. O'Hara."

He walked quickly to the ticket office. His legs didn't hurt at all.

CHAPTER SEVENTEEN

*W*HEN THE WEATHER became too wintry for Henry Jacoby to get his daily exercise (prescribed by his doctor, enforced by his wife) playing golf, he usually took a walk to the lighthouse. He usually took that walk just before noon.

Today as he swung down Cooke Street on his way home he looked at the shuttered Ryan house and he thought of his talk earlier with the journalist. What was his name? O'Mara? No, O'Hara, as in John O'Hara, one of his favorite writers, especially the short stories. He wondered how this O'Hara was making out with his own story.

The clock in the church tower bonged twelve. Dottie should be home from the hospital by now. He found her in the kitchen, unloading the contents of a market bag into cupboards and the refrigerator.

"Hello, Henry, good walk? Yes, I can see it was. You're absolutely oozing good health."

"You're looking fairly smashing yourself. Hard to believe you just came home from the hospital. Hey, funny coincidence today."

"On your way to the lighthouse? Meet a glowworm?"

"Happened here at home," Henry said. "A journalist named O'Hara stopped in to see me."

"That's a coincidence?"

"Interviewed me about the Barrow murder," Henry said. "That's half of the coincidence. The other half—"

"Is that I've been worrying about that very same murder. But why was this journalist interviewing you?"

"He's talking to all the neighbors. Trying to dig up some new angle. What did we see or hear or smell that night?"

"But you certainly couldn't tell him anything."

"Nary a thing."

"A pretty good coincidence," Dottie said, putting away the last of the groceries. "You couldn't tell O'Hara anything about the murder, and I can't tell you what's bothering me about it. Well, if we're going to have any lunch today, I'd better stir my stumps."

"What are we having for lunch, anyway?" Henry asked.

"Stumps," Dottie said.

Amy had finally drifted into a fitful sleep. Nancy lay watching the grim, unvarying light in the high window, listening to the only sound she could hear, the steady pounding of the surf on the beach below them. The bells in the Edgartown church didn't carry as far as the Goldsmith house, so she didn't know the time. But she knew it was too late to hope that Dave had decoded the message she had sent him over the phone. If he had, by now the police would have found her and Amy. Now the only hope of rescue lay in Amy.

How long, exactly, she wondered, had Amy been gone from home? Most of last night, at least, and all of this morning. Surely after this much time Claire and

Ken Lambert must be doing something about their missing daughter.

"What time do you think it is, Nancy?" Amy's voice was still full of sleep.

"It must be around noon," Nancy said. "Maybe even later."

"Maybe even one or two? Two o'clock until eight o'clock—that's six hours," Amy said, figuring. "And after David gives him the ransom, how soon do you think Andy will let us go?"

"Oh, pretty soon. An hour maybe."

"So in seven hours we could be out of here, right? And once I get home again, Nancy, I tell you I won't ever again . . . ."

"Ever again what, Amy?"

"Oh . . . nothing."

"Tell me, Amy. You won't ever again what?" Nancy tried to sound calm, merely interested. "Tell me how in the world you got into this? What were you doing here in the middle of the night?"

"Oh, I—I'd rather not . . . oh, okay. You'll find out anyway. Well, you see, Betty Lou Weaver and I—you know Betty Lou?"

"Yes. Go on."

"Well, Betty Lou and I—we like to have a drink now and then." And Amy told Nancy how she and Betty Lou had been riding out at night on their bikes and breaking into houses and stealing liquor. Until tonight, when Betty Lou had chickened out, and she had gone alone. "And when there wasn't any liquor in the Barnhardt house I thought of this place. Sally Goldsmith, she's a summer friend of mine, she says her grandmother gives loads of parties, so I thought there was sure to be some here. I broke a window to get in, and then I heard you yelling—"

"Amy, listen! Betty Lou knew where you were going, what you were going to do?"

"Well, sure. Like I said, she chickened out."

"But when you didn't come back last night, she would have told your mother, and *she* would go to the police."

"No," Amy said slowly, "I don't think so."

"Yes, she would!" Nancy insisted. "She'd be worried, Amy. And she'd tell the police you were looking for liquor in closed up houses and they'd start searching all those houses! Maybe they're getting close to us now. They may find us any minute!"

Amy was shaking her head again. "No, Nancy, I don't think that's going to happen. I guess we'll just have to wait until David pays the ransom and Andy lets us go."

"But why, Amy? When Betty Lou tells them—"

"That's just it, she won't tell them," Amy said miserably. "You don't know Betty Lou. Nobody ever had a more loyal friend than Betty Lou. Why, she'd die before she told them I was out stealing liquor! Wild horses couldn't drag it out of her."

It had dawned on David Webster in the middle of a sleepless night that Nancy's first call, having been a collect one, would have been recorded with the phone company. He had talked to the office when it opened in the morning; it took five minutes for him to get the information he wanted. The call, he was told, had been put through at eight-forty p.m.; it had lasted one minute. The number was 563-0405.

The kidnapper, Dave reasoned, wouldn't have called from a private house where the number could be so easily traced. But he dialed the number anyway and let it ring a dozen times before he hung up, sure that he had called a public phone, probably an outdoor booth. And in a place as small as Pocasset there wouldn't be many of those.

When the ferry had landed in Woods Hole, David, in Mrs. MacWilliams's car, was the third one off. He drove through Falmouth, then ten minutes north of it he turned off Route 28 toward Buzzards Bay. In another five minutes he was in Pocasset, looking for phone booths.

The first one he found was outside a Laundromat; its number wasn't the one he was looking for. Neither was the one in a booth beside a pharmacy. The third, at a closed gas station, was being used by a small boy whose bicycle leaned against the open door. He saw Dave and said into the phone, "I got to go now, somebody wants to make a call." He hung up and pushed his bike out of the way.

"Thanks, kid," Dave said.

"That's okay," the boy said, and rode off.

Dave stepped into the booth. The number on the phone was 563-0405.

He went outside and looked around him. The small boy was just pedaling around a curve in the road, and there was no one else in sight. But across the street, from a modest looking motel, came the sound of music. Dave went into the lobby; a man seated in an old wicker chair and watching television looked up at him, and smiled.

"Hello, there," he said, getting up to turn the sound down. "Hope you don't want a room. We're closed. Always close for the season right after Labor Day."

"No," Dave said, "I just want to talk to you for a minute."

143

"Sure thing. What can I do for you?"

"Were you here the night before last? Around nine o'clock?"

"Well, yes, it so happens I was. Right here in the lobby, me and my wife. We're the owners, you see, live here year round."

"I'm trying to track down a phone call that was made from that booth across the street. You can see it from here."

"That's right."

"A woman and a man made the call."

"Around nine o'clock, did you say?"

"Twenty of nine, to be exact."

"I didn't see anyone, but my wife did."

"She saw them? A man and a woman?"

"Yes. Thelma was at the window during a commercial, looking at the weather. That's how she happened to see those two people in the booth. And she saw the lady accidentally drop her scarf."

"Go on," David said.

"Thelma went rushing out and picked it up. Ran after them and gave it to the lady."

"Did your wife say anything about them? Did she talk to them?"

"I don't know. When Thelma came back her favorite TV show was starting. We didn't talk about it."

"Was there a car?" David asked. "Did she notice a car?"

"You'd have to ask Thelma about that."

"Is she here? May I talk to her?"

"She's over in Falmouth now, doing the marketing. Be back in another hour more or less, I'd say."

"I'll wait."

"Sure thing, sit down, make yourself comfortable."

The motelkeeper stuck out his hand. "My name's Elmer Myers."

David shook his hand and told him his name.

On his way back to the island O'Hara bought a beer and drank a toast to Ethel Winston. Then he bought another beer and drank to the fact that she was color blind. He had a third, and with it toasted Timothy O'Hara, capable detective.

As he drank the third beer he realized that something or other was vaguely bugging him. Something that was connected with Jim Barrow's murder. What was it, he wondered. A clue he had heard or seen, and missed? Was it a fact, or hearsay—something that someone had told him? Or a combination of both? He was still pondering when the ferry docked at Vineyard Haven.

He drove to Edgartown, re-registered at the Daggett House, and got his old room back. Once in that room he settled down in a comfortable chair to some intensive study.

Now what in hell was it, he asked himself, that was bugging him? It must have been something Ethel Winston had said to him on their ferry trip. He tried to recall their conversation. They had talked about her aged aunt in Falmouth...the possibility of his living on the Vineyard . . . his splendid necktie—Ethel had said she was going to buy one like it for her neighbor, Henry Jacoby. No, none of this could have anything to do with the Barrow murder. He was not making much headway.

Many people believed they thought better on their feet. O'Hara hadn't given that the try lately since it hurt him to be on his feet. He decided that now was the time. After a bit of limited pacing in the small room, without

145

his thinking improving any, he found himself at the window, looking down at the town dock, remembering his quaint dialogue with Jared Danbury, the ex-harbor master. Was it something Danbury had said? Could be. He would refer to his notes.

He dug his notebook out of his suitcase, found the page marked Danbury, and read his notes aloud.

"Danbury on Cooke Street the night of the murder," his notes ran. "Met Andy Fisher there. A. F. said he had been to the Fitzsimmons house, checking the furnace or something. . . ."

A bell rang in O'Hara's head. Excited, he quickly shuffled back to his early notes. Among the earliest he found what he was looking for; an interview with Andy Fisher. Andy had told him why he was in the Ryan neighborhood.

"A. F. said it had snowed that afternoon," he had written, "and he was afraid of a freeze. He worried about the furnace in the Fitzsimmons house, unreliable. At about nine that night, A. F. went to check it. It was okay."

Another bell rang for O'Hara. Twice in his notes the Fitzsimmons house was mentioned in connection with the murder. And today he had heard it still another time. Ethel was going to buy a necktie like his for her neighbor, Henry Jacoby. "They bought the old Fitzsimmons place across the street from me," she had told him. "Henry and Dottie, a darling couple."

A third bell rang and O'Hara recognized it—the jackpot!

The Fitzsimmons house was now owned and occupied by the Jacobys. But everyone, at least all the old-time islanders, still called it the Fitzsimmons house. So when Andy claimed he was checking the furnace in the Fitzsimmons house, he was actually referring to the Jacoby house.

And now at last O'Hara had it. He had put it together. Henry Jacoby had been holed up for two days in that house, writing a speech. He had been there on the night of the murder. No way Andy Fisher could have gone into that house and checked the furnace, not without encountering Jacoby.

So Andy Fisher was lying.

But why was he lying? What did he have to hide? Interesting questions, O'Hara thought. He was too hopped up to stay in his room, he had to get out and about. Grabbing his coat, he went down the stairs and out of the hotel. Maybe he would think more clearly in the open air.

It wasn't safe nowadays, Marion Weaver thought indignantly, to come to the supermarket. The prices were enough to give an economy-minded housewife ulcers. The meat, for instance, at which she was now staring sadly— well, from now on the Weaver family was going to go Italian, and eat a lot of pasta. Spaghetti, macaroni, noodles, fettuccini, lasagne. She pushed her cart to the pasta section and found that Claire Lambert had beat her to it.

"Good-by, meat," Marion said, "hello, spaghetti. God's answer to inflation."

"You're so right," Claire said. "I was trying to remember the last time I had a lamb chop. Is my daughter a charming house guest?"

"Amy is always a charming house guest."

"What are the girls up to this afternoon?"

Puzzled, Marion said, "But they're not together, Claire. Betty Lou's next door at the Dairy Queen, having something fattening before lunch. Amy went home early this morning."

"She didn't come home," Claire said. "I haven't seen her since yesterday."

147

"But Betty Lou said . . . look, she's going to wait for me in the car. Let's go see her."

The two mothers arrived at the car just as Betty Lou was about to go back to the Dairy Queen for something else fattening before lunch.

"Hi, Mrs. Lambert," she said.

"Dear," Marion said, "when Amy left this morning, did she say she was going home?"

"Well . . . not exactly," Betty Lou said. Then she said quickly to Amy's mother, "Didn't she? Isn't she home?"

"No, not yet. What time did she leave, Betty Lou?"

"Well . . . I don't know exactly."

"So you didn't look at the clock," Marion Weaver said, slightly impatient. "Was it right after it got light, or before it got light, or when?"

"I don't know," Betty Lou said, looking frightened. "She —well, she left before I woke up. So I don't know what time it was."

"Then why on earth," her mother said, "did you tell me she had gone home?"

"Because I thought—where else would she go?"

Claire Lambert shook her head. "I have no idea. Anyplace—everyplace. She should have phoned. It's a rule that she always tell us where she is. Well, I'd better start phoning around."

"Mrs. Lambert. . . ."

"Yes, dear?"

"I think maybe. . . ." She stopped. She looked now as if she were about to cry. "I'm sorry."

"It's not your fault, dear. But it is thoughtless of Amy."

Betty Lou watched Amy's mother cross the parking lot to her car, and she almost did burst into tears, she was that upset and nervous. She had almost told Amy's mother where Amy had gone. She had caught herself just in time. She knew what would happen if she ever told; Amy would never forgive her, never in a million years. Amy wouldn't even speak to her again, let alone be her best friend. And Betty Lou couldn't bear to let that happen. So, she warned herself, she must never tell. Wild horses wouldn't drag it out of her.

CHAPTER EIGHTEEN

"*T*HERE SHE IS NOW!" An old station wagon was turning into the motel driveway, rolling past the lobby entrance. "Thelma's back," Elmer Myers said. "I'll unload the groceries while you talk to her. You wait right here."

A few minutes later a short stout woman came bustling into the lobby, smiling, holding out a mittened hand. She wore tight, bright blue ski pants, and a turtle neck sweater that matched her rosy cheeks. She exhaled good health, good will, and good spirits.

"Hello, there, Mr. Webster," she said, shaking his hand warmly. "Elmer says you want to talk to me."

"Yes. About the couple you saw in the phone booth the night before last."

"Sure!" Plopping down on a leather hassock, which hissed softly under her weight, she hiked a pack of cigarettes from a pants pocket, lighted one with a kitchen match, and smiled at him through a cloud of smoke. "I was looking out that window and I saw the lady drop her scarf. I went and got it, went after them and gave it to her. They were walking awfully fast, I had to run to catch up to them. Does that help you any?"

"I know the woman," David said. "What can you tell me about the man?"

"I can't help you much there," she said, shaking her head. "I never really got a look at his face."

"How tall was he? Was he thin, or stocky, or what?"

"Well," she said, trying to remember, "he wasn't very tall. Not much taller than I am. He was kind of a sturdy fellow with a mackinaw and a cap—"

"Did he talk? Did you hear his voice?"

"He did say something, but I couldn't understand him. I think the poor man must have been pretty drunk."

"Drunk!" David said, stunned. "You thought he was *drunk*?"

"Well, if you could see the trouble he had walking—practically staggering he was. The lady seemed to be holding him up."

"Did you see where they were headed? Did they get in a car?"

"No, I didn't see where they went," Thelma said. "But I remember thinking that if they did have a car, I hoped she would do the driving. He was in no condition to drive."

When Ken Lambert heard the car door slam he went to the window. Claire was coming across the lawn alone. When he saw her face he hurried to the door.

"Claire! What is it?"

"I couldn't find her."

"My God, the way you looked, I thought . . . Claire, darling, you've got to pull yourself together. You're exaggerating this whole thing."

"No. I've been all over town looking for Amy. All the places she ever goes to; no one has seen her today. I even phoned the hospital, but, thank God, she isn't there. Oh, where is she? What's happened to her?"

151

"Claire," Ken said, "Amy is a big girl. She can take care of herself. She's off somewhere on her bicycle, Oak Bluffs, maybe, or up-island. Remember, she did exactly the same thing a couple of years ago. And she came home safe and sound before dark. Remember how worried you were? All for nothing."

"I'm going to call the police," Claire said.

"You haven't been listening to me. Please *listen* to me."

"I heard you. Amy has done this before, you said. But she realized how upset I was, and she promised never to do it again."

"That was quite a while ago," Ken said. "Little girls forget their promises."

"You said Amy was a big girl, and she is," Claire said. "Big girls don't forget their promises." Claire stood up, then sank back onto the sofa. "I can't do it. Will you call them?"

"Claire, darling," Ken said. "Calling the police—it's going to be embarrassing for Amy when she comes waltzing in here in the next hour."

"The next hour," Claire said. "All right, we'll wait an hour, then we'll call the police. Won't we, Ken? Please?"

"All right," Ken said.

O'Hara had been on the top deck of the town dock for some time, alternately pacing and just sitting and thinking. The day was so cold, the wind so raw, he had the whole place to himself. Now, as he neared the completion of his seventh lap, he slowed down, slammed his right fist triumphantly into his left hand and said aloud, "Got it! Everything but the motive. Yes, sir, got it all—everything but the motive!"

He went through it all again, mentally writing the report he would eventually turn in to his office.

A. Andy Fisher had been the Ryans' gardener and caretaker since Nancy was a child. He would have had a key to the house of course; after the Ryans' sudden death he could have kept the key and had access to the house at any time. And

B. had known what was in the house. Know that Nancy's father's gun was still there, and where it was kept. Known about the jewelry.

C. He could have used his key to enter the house and kill Jim Barrow. Could have hidden the jewelry where it was certain to be found. Could have opened a back window through which the murderer supposedly escaped. And then, while he buried the gun in the flower box, he could have worn one of Nancy's scarves and a coat, just on the chance he might be seen, as indeed he was. Then he could have returned the coat and slipped out into the night, where

D. He was seen by Mr. Jared Danbury, retired harbor master. And to whom he lied about his presence in the neighborhood.

E. He then went to the police and told them that he had seen a strange man in the Ryan backyard. A story he must have known they wouldn't believe. But a story that, in case any suspicion should ever fall on him, would certainly remove it. It would only prove his loyalty to his longtime friend, Nancy Ryan.

And the last point on O'Hara's list was the fact that Andy Fisher was not a tall man, not more than five foot, five, not quite as tall as Nancy. He could have, O'Hara believed, been mistaken for her at the flower box.

Yes, O'Hara thought, Andy could certainly have murdered Jim Barrow, but why? What was his motive? And why would he want Nancy accused and tried, and probably convicted of murder?

There were questions that needed answering and

O'Hara thought that if he was half the detective that at this moment he considered himself to be, he would dig up the answes. His first step might be a further talk with Andy himself. Nothing accusatory, of course, just a casual chat, during which Andy might reveal why he hated Nancy Webster so much he wanted her convicted of murder. But before he talked to Andy he had a phone call to make.

From the booth on the corner he dialed his office in Boston. Cap Andrews himself, head of the Andrews Investigating Service, answered the phone.

"Cap?" O'Hara said. "O'Hara here."

"Back in town already?"

"No, I'm still in Edgartown."

"Why?"

"I met a key witness in the trial on the ferry. I got some new information that is going to clear Nancy Webster of the murder. And I got me a suspect I'm on my way to see right now."

"Well, well, kid, you're sounding like the former Tim O'Hara."

"I could wrap this scene up in a couple of hours. By tomorrow, anyway."

"Make it no later than tomorrow," Cap said. "I got a new assignment for you, starting Monday. Nice going, kid."

Cap hung up. So did O'Hara, asking himself if Cap had actually mentioned his next assignment. As of Monday? As of Monday he was not fired? He decided that the answer was in his favor.

He looked at his watch. It was still too early to go to Ethel's house. That was a visit he was looking forward to. Maybe it, too, would turn out in his favor. Maybe Ethel would accept his invitation to dinner at the Kelley House tonight.

CHAPTER NINETEEN

O<small>N THEIR WINTER</small> schedule the ferries made fewer crossings than they did the rest of the year, and the next boat for the Vineyard didn't leave until three forty-five. David drove slowly back to Woods Hole, disappointed and depressed. His one hope, that this trip to a phone booth in Pocasset would lead him to Nancy, had been smashed.

Well, he asked himself, what in God's name had he expected of Thelma Myers? That she would give him such a complete description of the kidnapper that he might recognize him? Or that she could tell him the license number of the car he had been driving? And whether they had been headed north or west, or perhaps back to Woods Hole, and the ferry?

For it occurred to him now, as it had before, that the collect call from Pocasset might have been meant to mislead him, to make him believe that Nancy was being held on the Cape. When it was quite likely she had been taken straight back to the Vineyard.

Then, for the millionth time he thought of Nancy's call last night. Her voice changing, rising; pretending that the connection was bad, that he hadn't heard her. Repeating words she had already said loud and clear. ". . . wait until the picture is over, stay in the middle of the third row until it has ended. . . ." Asking again if he could hear her. ". . . you couldn't hear me, David?" Insisting that he get her message. ". . . And now do you hear me? And now do you?"

But what the hell had the message been? He had gone over those lines again and again. He had gone back in their lives, through all their summers together, trying to figure it out. *The end of the picture. . . the third row. . . the middle of the third row. . . .* The words meant nothing to him. He couldn't think of anything that would explain Nancy's S O S, if that's what it had been.

Of course it had been an S O S. Think, stupid, think!

Andy was checking their bonds when Nancy heard the car in the distance. It was coming closer; its tires had left the dirt road and were crunching gravel before Andy became aware of it. He leapt to his feet and stood, blinking, long enough for Nancy to pray that the driver would see Andy's blue pickup; long enough for her then to remember that he always hid it behind the old carriage house.

The car had stopped. Its doors opened and closed, and the sound galvanized Andy into action. He pulled open the storeroom door, yanked the key from the lock, eased the door closed, and locked it from the inside. Crouching beside Amy, he grasped her by a handful of her long hair. The knife was in his other hand, and its point was at her throat. He looked at both of them. He didn't have to say anything. They understood.

Downstairs the front door squeaked open, and Nancy heard the sound of several voices, the words undistinguishable. They rose and faded as the speakers moved through the rooms on the lower floor. Then, as the group mounted the stairs, she recognized one voice.

"...and it's available through Labor Day," Mickey Jamison was saying, in her bright, cheerful way. "The Goldsmiths are spending the summer abroad. Lucky you, Mrs. and Mr. McGrath."

"And the rent is ...?" a man's voice asked. "Are Nell and I lucky about that?"

"Oh, yes, I think so," Mickey said. "It's six thousand, including the utilities."

Andy Fisher could hardly believe his ears. In the eighteen years he had been the Goldsmiths' caretaker, they had never rented their house. No one enjoyed summers on the island as much as they did. That darned Mrs. Jamison, he thought angrily, she should not be showing this house to people. That darned Mrs. Jamison was making a mistake, she had got some names mixed up or something, and if she spoiled his plans, if she interfered with them at all ... he heard Amy gasp and he glanced down at her. In his rage at Mickey Jamison he had pressed down on the knife, and a fleck of Amy's blood stained the point of its blade. He relaxed his hand, but the knife was still at her throat as he listened to the intruders move about the house.

"Just look at the view from this window!" Mickey was saying. "Katama Bay and Chappaquiddick! This view alone is worth the rent."

"It is lovely," the other lady said. "How many bedrooms are there?"

"I'm not quite sure," Mickey said. "But we'll soon find out."

Their voices faded again as the party moved in and out of the many bedrooms. Then they stopped in front of the storage room and the lady was saying, "What's in here?"

Nancy saw the doorknob turn, heard it rattle back and forth, and the lady said, "Oh, it's locked. Is it another bedroom, Mrs. Jamison? I do hope so. Our kids want to have loads of guests, all summer."

"I'm not sure what it is," Mickey said, "but I have some keys in the car. One of them is sure to fit."

Mr. McGrath spoke then. "Don't bother, Mrs. Jamison, I don't think—"

"No bother," Mickey said, her voice fading as her heels tapped down the hall, down the stairway. "I'll only be a minute."

"I'm going to have another look at the kitchen," Mrs. McGrath said to her husband. "Want to come along?"

"No, thank you," her husband said. "I've seen enough kitchens for one day."

Nancy heard footsteps on the stairs again. Outside the door she heard the scratch of a match, then the smell of cigarette smoke drifted through. She turned her eyes away from the door to look at Andy. His gaze was fastened on her, but the knife was still pressed against Amy's throat.

In a few minutes Mickey Jamison and Mrs. McGrath were coming up the stairs together. Nancy could hear the jingle of keys.

"Now, we'll just try these," Mickey was saying, "and in a minute—"

"Mrs. Jamison," Mr. McGrath said, interrupting firmly, "I'm sorry, but I've decided that the rent here is a little too high. Now if you happen to have something as large, but a little less expensive—"

"You bet I do!" Mickey said, unfazed, cheerful and buoyant as ever. "The Dickens house on Starbuck Lane! Oh, you're just going to love the Dickens house. . . ."

Evan Weaver was, this late afternoon in November, inspecting his property, not without pride. His house was, with its unpainted weathered shingles, a blessing undisguised in this time of inflation. Ken Lambert, whose house had needed a paint job last spring, Evan remembered, had almost been driven to write an editorial accusing the island painters of price-gouging, comparing them with OPEC. The only painting needed on the Weaver place was a touchup on the window and door frames every few years, and that Evan could do himself. Then his mind went back to the Lamberts.

Claire Lambert was ordinarily a sensible, charming, completely attractive woman. But, as a mother, skip the word sensible. For her to call the police this afternoon and report her daughter missing was overreacting. Certainly Amy would be turning up before dark.

He switched his attention from the Lamberts to his driveway. The gravel was getting a little sparse in spots. Well, he would take care of that next spring. He walked around to the back yard and smiled at the sight of the tree house he had built for Betty Lou as soon as she was old enough to climb a ladder. He examined it. Did it need paint? No. Was it safe? It looked secure from down here. He climbed the ladder to make sure, and he was sure. He had built the tree house well. Looking around, he noted that Betty Lou was a good tree-house-keeper. Everything was in order, neat and clean.

Then he saw something that made him laugh, something that Betty Lou had tried unsuccessfully to hide. A small stack of comic books.

Last summer he and Marion had suggested that Betty Lou was too elderly, sophisticated, and beautiful to still be reading those little kids' comic books. Flattered, Betty Lou had promised that once she had read them all one last time she would throw them away. But evidently it had been a habit not that easily broken. Apparently Betty Lou had had withdrawal pains that were too much for her. Apparently she was having to taper off her comic book addiction gradually.

He stopped to pick one up. He would have a little fun with Betty Lou, tease her a bit. Tomorrow at their Sunday morning breakfast he would pretend to be reading this comic book with great interest and excitement. Then he saw a name in a childish scrawl on its cover. The name was not Betty Lou Weaver. It was Mary Elizabeth Friedlander.

He knew that name, he had heard it recently. Yes, yesterday morning he had read a story in the *Gazette*. The police were certain that teenagers were involved in the theft of liquor from closed houses. Bicycle tracks had been found at several of those houses and, recently, the Friedlander house had been broken into and some comic books had been taken.

Whoever had stolen liquor from the Friedlander house, Evan thought with a sinking heart, had also stolen Mary Elizabeth's comic books.

David knew the deckhand who directed his car into its parking place on the ferry. When Dave was a kid he had often fished the bridges on the Edgarton road beside him. What young Dave knew about fishing he had learned from his grown-up mentor, Fred Nelson.

"Hey, Davey," Fred said, coming to the window," I got something really rich to tell you. See you in the lunchroom, okay?"

"Okay, Fred," Dave said. "I'll see you up there."

But David stayed in his car. He spent the forty-minute voyage concentrating again on Nancy's phone call. "... *wait till the picture is over ... the third row ... stay in the third row ....*"

He had sworn to himself that before the ferry made its right-angle turn around the buoy into Vineyard Haven harbor, he would have decoded her cry for help, but he hadn't.

"Just happened to see you here, Davey," Fred Nelson said, standing again beside the window. "Sorry I couldn't make it to the lunchroom."

"That's all right, Fred," David said.

"Got a story to tell you," Fred said, grinning. "The other night, on our last trip, we had old Andy Fisher and his pickup on board. You know Andy, don't you?"

"Sure," David said.

"Sure, everybody knows old Andy. Now, get this! We land, Andy is in his pickup, it's his turn to move out. He turns on the ignition, he steps on the gas. Nothing! His battery is dead as a doornail." Fred chuckled happily. "Well, after all the cars are off, we push him off and we start kidding him, you know, putting him on, having fun. But now, Davey, here's the funny part. When we push the truck off I seen something move—"

"Hey, Fred!" an angry voice shouted. "Get the hell *with* it, will you? Let's get these doors the hell open so the folks can get the hell off!"

"Sorry," Fred said to David, "I got to make a living. Tell you the rest the next time I see you. Okay, Davey?"

"Okay," David said.

CHAPTER TWENTY

EITHER HE HAD BEEN given a bum steer or he had misunderstood the directions. Whichever, O'Hara was lost. He was parked now at an intersection on the outskirts of town, hoping someone would come along to help him. Someone soon did; a boy on a bicycle delivering papers.

"Hey, kid," O'Hara said, "do you happen to deliver one of those papers to Andy Fisher?"

"No, sir," the boy said. "Why?"

O'Hara laughed and said, "I was hoping you could tell me where he lives."

"I can. Last house on Grove Street."

"Now I'm hoping you can tell me where Grove Street is."

"Easy," the boy said, pointing straight ahead. "First left, then next right is Grove Street. Andy's house is at the end of the street, all by itself."

Night had fallen and Andy's house, illuminated only by the headlights of O'Hara's car, was a sorry sight, a small, ramshackle cottage. It was unlighted and there was no blue pickup in sight—convincing enough evidence that Andy was not at home. Should he stay in his car, O'Hara wondered, and wait for him? Or should be unlawfully enter Andy's house and see what he could find? Something incriminating, for instance. More than once in his career he had done that, and found what he was looking for. O'Hara made up his mind.

He backed out of Grove Street; parked his car where, should Andy see it on his way home, he would not connect it with a visitor to his house. He took his flashlight from the glove compartment and went back to the house. He found the front door locked. Efficiently locked. He walked around to the back of the house and there his flashlight picked out a stone wall. It was an impressive wall, six or seven feet high, with a door in it that was firmly padlocked. He found an old crate, dragged it to the wall and climbed up onto it.

What he saw on the other side was a ruin, the ruin of what once must have been a fabulous garden, with a fountain and a pond and marble benches. Now it was a neglected wasteland, a jungle. Andy must have made this garden, spent years making it, and then tired of it. Why, O'Hara wondered, had he abandoned it?

The back door, he found, was easy, a cinch. He opened it with his American Express card. Don't leave home without it. Don't go to someone else's home without it.

Once inside it took but a minute or two to case the place. One floor, four rooms. His initial rapid examination told him two things about Andy Fisher.

In a corner of the kitchen was a cage full of rabbits. Well cared for pets, they were sleek and fat. Item one, Andy liked animals. Significant? Hardly.

The only reading matter in the house was on a single subject. A glass-doored bookcase was crammed with books, hard-cover and paperback, manuals and magazines, all devoted to gardening, to the growing of flowers

163

only. Item two, Andy loved flowers. Significant? Again, hardly.

So the only two facts that O'Hara had gleaned from breaking into the house were of no help to him. But after all he'd only been in the place a few minutes. Work a little harder, O'Hara told O'Hara. He concentrated on the parlor. On that glass-doored bookcase. He started looking through it carefully, and after a few minutes, found something that did not pertain to either rabbits or flowers. It pertained to Andy Fisher. Andy Fisher, himself, his life and times.

"Darling!" Dottie Jacoby said suddenly, "I've got it!"

"Thank God!" Henry Jacoby said.

"I've put it all together!"

"Great, now maybe you'll stop acting like a zombie."

"You were here the night of the murder."

"Correct."

"That clipping I threw away quoted Andy Fisher. He told the police he was in the neighborhood that night to check the furnace in the Fitzsimmons house."

"Now you've lost me," Henry said.

"*This* is the Fitzsimmons house!"

"To lots of people, yes. So?"

"So why did Andy say such a thing?"

"Now I'm with you," Henry said. "Andy didn't check any furnace in this house that night."

"Could he have done it without you hearing him?"

"Absolutely not."

"So why did he say he did? And what do we do about it?"

"Maybe nothing," Henry said.

"When somebody lies about a murder," Dottie said, "the police should be told."

"The trial is long over," Henry said, "and Nancy was

164

acquitted. But let's think about it. As we used to say on Madison Avenue, let's toss it in the food processor and see how it shreds."

Officer Jimmy Corto looked up from his desk when Police Chief Danzig put down his phone and was finally free for a minute. "Hey, Chief," he said. "Any reason for me to stick around now?"

"Saturday night, huh? Got a date? Going up to Gay Head?"

"Yeah, I'm bringing Sandy down-island to have dinner at the Dunes. Then we're going to the movies."

"You've got a lot of traveling to do, Jimmy. Get on your horse."

"Is that an order, Chief?"

"That's an order, son. Get going."

The door to the office opened and Evan Weaver came in, his young daughter in tow. "Good evening, Chief," he said. "Betty Lou has something to tell you. About Amy Lambert."

"Amy Lambert's been reported missing," the Chief said. "Is that what you have something to tell me about, Betty Lou?"

"Yes," Betty Lou said, her voice just a whisper. "She— Amy came to stay at my house last night. We were going to break into an empty house and we were going to—oh, Daddy!" she cried, turning to him, imploringly.

He shook his head, his face stern. "Go on, Betty Lou."

She took a deep breath and spilled it all out as fast as she could, so she could get it over with. "We were going to steal some liquor and we knew where there was some because we'd been to that house before but I got scared and wouldn't go so Amy went by herself. On her bike."

"What time did she go?"

"Eleven—a little after eleven o'clock."

165

"Eleven o'clock last night? She's been gone since then?" The child's mother had reported she'd been gone since early this morning; it had not been considered an emergency then. Now it was a different matter. Danzig reached across his desk for the radio mike. "What house was she going to?"

"The Barnhardts," Betty Lou said.

The Chief switched on the mike. He instructed Lou Quigley in patrol car number one to investigate the Barnhardt house out on the airport road, on the chance that the missing child, Amy Lambert, might be there. Lou Quigley's voice crackled back that he was only a minute or two away from the Barnhardt house, and he would be reporting back in no time.

"Chief," Jimmy Corto said from his desk, "she wouldn't have found any liquor there last night."

"No?" Danzig said.

"The Barnhardts were up last weekend, remember? They reported that a window had been broken and some liquor taken. They had the window repaired and took what liquor was left back to Providence."

"Did you do that, Betty Lou?" Danzig asked. "You and your friend Amy?"

Miserably, tongue-tied, she nodded.

Jesus, the Chief thought to himself, those two little girls. Such little kids. He'd thought it had been boys, juniors or seniors in high school. But these two little girls, hardly into their teens . . . he shook his head.

In less than five minutes the receiver on his desk came alive. Officer Lou Quigley was reporting from his patrol car.

"It looks as though she's been here," he said. "A kitchen window's been broken. And there are bike tracks up the lane to the house and back. But the house is empty."

"Stay where you are, Lou, I'll get back to you," Danzig

166

said, then turned to the Weavers. "What would Amy do, Betty Lou? She didn't find anything to take in that house, so what would she do?"

The sharpness in his tone, the urgency, frightened Betty Lou. "I—I don't know," she said, lips trembling. "Maybe she—Oh,I don't know!"

"Think about it," Danzig said, more softly, trying to conceal his apprehension. "How would Amy feel when she found there wasn't any liquor there? Very disappointed? Angry? How?"

"She would be mad," Betty Lou said.

"She wanted to find some pretty badly?"

"She could hardly wait for last night. She kept talking about it all the time."

"So do you think she might break into some other house? Where she might find liquor?"

"Maybe," Betty Lou said, timidly trying to help, "she would go back to one of the houses we'd already been to. You know, so she could be pretty sure there would be some there."

"That's a good idea," Danzig said, encouraging her. "Whose houses have you gone into?"

"The Davallions' house," Betty Lou said, not looking at him or her father; looking at the floor. "And the Malloys' and the Tillers' and the Greens'."

If Amy had gone into one of those houses, Danzig thought, and was still in it, then something had happened to her. Some accident had trapped her there, preventing her from going home. Or, he wondered grimly, how strong was the child's alcohol habit? Strong enough so that if she found a bottle she might drink enough to become ill or pass out? God, he hoped not. But whatever had happened, he knew it wasn't good.

"Chief," Jimmy Corto said, interrupting Danzig's disturbing thoughts. "Why don't I check the Tiller house,

167

and the Malloys? Lou can check the other two."

"What about your date?"

"I'll stick around," Jimmy said. "I figure you can use some extra help."

"Okay," the Chief said. "Get going, Jimmy."

Jimmy got going. Danzig relayed the names of the other two houses to Lou Quigley and Lou Quigley got going. Then Danzig told Evan Weaver that he and his daughter might also leave. He promised to let them know as soon as Amy was found.

Then, reluctantly, he picked up the phone and dialed Ken Lambert's number. It was his unhappy duty to report to Ken that his missing daughter was one of the children who had been breaking into closed houses and stealing liquor. He thought of the piece that Ken had written for the *Gazette* yesterday, at their suggestion.

Ethel Winston parked her Volvo in the garage. She walked across the breezeway to the kitchen briskly, a woman anxious to get where she was going. Inside the house, before even dropping her purse or shedding her jacket, she turned on the burner under the kettle. In a few minutes, a cup of hot tea in hand, she was forcing herself to sit back in a kitchen chair, not on the very edge of it.

Her aunt had been right. Ethel's mind had been entirely centered on Timothy O'Hara, private detective, and what he was doing to clear Nancy Webster of the clinging suspicion of murder.

She looked at the kitchen clock. Quarter of five. Just fifteen minutes to wait until he would be here. She wondered if he had found the murderer, if he had gone to Nancy with the news. She had seen David Webster as he drove off the homecoming ferry that afternoon; in the glimpse she had of him she thought he looked tense and tired. Well, Mr. O'Hara's news would surely be welcomed by both him and Nancy.

She looked at the clock again. Only ten minutes to wait now.

CHAPTER TWENTY-ONE

O<small>N HIS WAY BACK</small> to the Goldsmith house Andy made a stop at the market to buy cold cuts and milk and chocolate bars. The store was nearly empty and only Bert Crouse, a scallop fisherman, was at the checkout counter.

"Say, Andy," Bert said as the girl was bagging his order. "You know that writer fellow going around town, asking about the Barrow murder?"

Andy nodded. "Yes, he talked to me."

"Oh, I guess he found your house all right, then."

"Found my house?"

"Yeah," Bert said, pocketing his change. "I was outside the drug store about half an hour ago. He was asking us where you lived and we told him. He's probably waiting for you at your place now."

"Thanks, Bert," Andy said.

Andy paid his bill, picked up his bag of groceries and went out to his truck.

When O'Hara realized that what he had come upon pertained to Andy Fisher himself, he had gone into the kitchen, at the back of the house, where he could use his flashlight without its being seen from the road. He placed the thick cardboard-covered notebook he had found on the table. On its cover was printed MY SCRAPBOOK, under it in sprawling letters was written "Andy Fisher."

Centered on the first page was a yellowed newspaper clipping; it had been printed in the *Gazette* over twenty-five years before. The story included a photo of a grinning schoolboy proudly displaying an enormous fish. Andy Fisher, at the age of fourteen, had won second prize in the annual fisherman's derby. The fish was a thirty-two-pound striped bass. That seemed to have been Andy's sole teenage triumph.

On the next page was a story, again accompanied by a photo, a picture of a grown-up Andy, posing with a stout, middle-aged woman. The story mentioned Andy Fisher was the woman's gardener, and that she was Mrs. Halstead Norton, whose rose garden had been featured in that month's *House and Garden.* O'Hara turned another page and his interest quickened as he looked at a picture of a smiling and very young Nancy Ryan. She had finished first in the backstroke race in the ten-year-old class.

From then on the book could have been Nancy Ryan's own scrapbook. There were clippings about her when she crewed in the island regatta, when she worked as a candy-striper in the hospital, when she and David Webster won the junior mixed doubles at the yacht club finals. Her picture had been in the paper when she had been accepted as a freshman at Dana Hall, and as a bridesmaid in a June wedding at the Whalers' church. Page after page chronicled the summertime activities of a girl named Nancy Ryan.

O'Hara turned still another page, and his breath exploded in a gasp of disbelief. He was looking at a photo of Nancy, and another of Andy Fisher. There was no story, only a headline. The headline read: NANCY RYAN MARRIED TO ANDY FISHER.

O'Hara told himself his flashlight was failing—he had misread the headline because of the inadequate light. He zoomed in his flashlight, pinpointing the words and the photos and suddenly, staring at them, he understood. He understood not only the newspaper clipping, but also at last, the motive for Jim Barrow's murder. For the announcement of the Nancy Ryan-Andy Fisher wedding had, of course, never appeared in any paper. It was simply a collage, dreamed up by Andy, designed by him, the pictures clipped from old *Gazettes*, the words made of letters cut from the paper and pasted together.

Now O'Hara was able to add it all up, and in a sad and terrible way it all made sense. Ever since Nancy was a child, Andy had fantasized their future—one day they would marry, and live happily ever after. It would probably explain that grotesquerie of a garden. Andy could have built it for Nancy while he waited for his bride to come of age, come back to the island and marry him. But when she came it was with a husband.

O'Hara thought he could imagine Andy's feelings, what it would mean to this simple-minded gardener, this childish keeper of pet rabbits. Shock, disbelief, then outraged fury that his dream had been stolen from him, and stolen by Nancy herself. There would be an absolute need to get revenge, to hurt her as much as she had hurt him. If he murdered her husband—no, it must hurt her more than that. It must destroy her. If he murdered her husband and made the police think she had done it? Then she would be sent to prison for the rest of her life. Yes, that would be the way Andy would reason, that would be the sort of revenge he would demand.

O'Hara was ready now to go to the police. There was no doubt in his mind he could convince them that Andy

172

Fisher was guilty of Jim Barrow's murder. As far as he was concerned the case was solved and closed.

There was one more filled page remaining in the scrapbook. The *Gazette* photograph showed the Edgartown harbor, shot from behind a crowd of people, all facing out to sea. There the hulk of a fire-blackened sloop was being towed into the boatyard. Andy had included no text with this clipping. There was only the photo with one of his homemade headlines, formed by pasting together letters. This one read: ANDY FISHER BLOWS UP RYAN BOAT.

O'Hara's hands were trembling as he closed the book. The terrible story was complete. Andy had been proud of what he had done, he had recorded it in his scrapbook. Obviously he had felt that Nancy's parents would stand in the way of their marriage, and he had murdered them to prevent that. Andy Fisher, the dedicated gardener he had thought so childish and simple, was a shrewd and calculating monster. Carrying the book under his arm, O'Hara got out of the house as quickly as he could.

He made his way back to his car, got in, put the scrapbook on the seat beside him. He had just slid the key into the ignition, when he felt hands clutch at his throat, close savagely around it. The hands tightened like the iron jaws of a vice, and very soon the life of Timothy O'Hara had ended.

Carefully, Andy got out of the back seat, opened the driver's door, and pushed the still figure out from under the wheel. He took its place, started the car and drove at a steady and moderate speed to the edge of a small, deep, inland pond he knew, no more than half a mile away. The speedometer needle was pointing to thirty when Andy jumped out of the moving car. He watched it sink out of sight in the murky water. He stood by the pond only a minute or two, then turned and started hiking briskly through the woods back to town.

"Did you talk to them, Henry?" Dottie Jacoby said as Henry walked in the door. "What did they say? What are they going to do about it?"

"Yes," Henry said, "I talked to them. Or rather to Chief Danzig. He was interested. He made a note of it."

"And they'll talk to Andy, won't they? Find out why he lied?"

"They'll check it out, but at the moment they have an emergency on their hands."

"Oh, Henry, what?"

"Amy Lambert's missing."

"What do you mean, missing? Lost, or run away, or what?"

"All I know is that she hasn't been seen since about eleven last night."

"Henry, that's terrible! Oh, poor Claire and Ken, they must be out of their minds."

CHAPTER TWENTY-TWO

*W*HEN OFFICERS Corto and Quigley had finished searching their assigned houses and radioed in their failure to find the missing girl, the Chief ordered them back to headquarters. There they found him and Officer Al Potter huddled over a detailed street map of Edgartown.

"The child," Danzig told them, glancing up from the map, "is probably in one of the closed houses in town. We'll go through each of them until she's found."

"My God," Lou Quigley said, "how many of those houses are there? Hundreds, right? We'll need help."

"Help is on its way," Danzig said. "Oak Bluff's sending a car, and so is Tisbury. They'll cover Clam Bay and the airport road. Lou, you take the houses on Planting Field Way . . . Al, the ones on Starbuck Neck and North Water."

The two policemen nodded, turned, and left the office. Outside, as they got into their squad cars, Ethel Winston swerved her car into the parking lot and slammed on the brakes.

Inside Jimmy Corto said, "Chief, I've got an idea. That list we have of houses empty for the winter—a lot of them have caretakers. We've got their names, and they all have keys—"

"I'm with you, Jimmy. Good thinking."

The Chief immediately found the list in a top drawer of his desk. At a quick look there appeared to be a dozen or so caretakers, some of them with as many as five or six, some with even eight or nine houses in their charge. With their cooperation, Danzig thought, we might be able to eliminate fifty or sixty houses from our search.

The door opened. The Chief looked up as Ethel Winston came into the office, and knew that more trouble was in store for the Edgartown police that night.

He had known Mrs. Winston for many years, a serene and smiling, down-to-earth, no-nonsense sort of person. Not the sort to burst into police headquarters of an evening with a face as anxious and eyes as troubled as hers were tonight.

"Good evening, Mrs. Winston," he said. "Is something wrong?"

"I'm afraid so, Chief."

Danzig handed the list of caretakers to Jimmy. "Start on this, Jimmy," he said. "Tell them the places our men are covering, so they won't waste their time checking them."

Jimmy Corto nodded and took the list to a desk in the corner. He pulled the phone toward him and began dialing. Danzig turned his attention to Ethel.

"Chief," she said, "there's a man in town now, a Timothy O'Hara—does that name mean anything to you?"

"Yes. He was in to see me the other day."

"I thought he might have been in touch with you this afternoon. About the extraordinary discovery he's made concerning the Barrow murder case." At his desk, Jimmy Corto hung up the phone, and he and the Chief exchanged glances; this was the second time in only a few hours the subject of the Barrow murder had been brought up.

Danzig said, "No, he hasn't talked to me today."

"I am deeply concerned about him. I'm afraid he may be in trouble."

176

"Why?"

"He's made a breakthrough in the Barrow murder. He is able to prove that Nancy Webster is innocent." The skeptical look that the Chief couldn't hide prompted Ethel instantly to try to convince him. "You remember my testimony at the trial, Chief Danzig? How damaging it was to Nancy? I said I saw her remain at that window box long enough for her to have buried a gun."

"Yes, I remember."

"The person I saw there was not Nancy, it was the murderer. And Mr. O'Hara can prove that."

In the corner Jimmy Corto hung up the phone and dialed another number.

"Mrs. Winston," the Chief was saying, "I can appreciate your feelings, how anxious you are to believe this development. But Mr. O'Hara is a writer, looking for some new angle on this story, he—"

"But that's just it," Ethel said. "Mr. O'Hara is not a writer. He is a private investigator, working for an agency in Boston. He was hired to investigate this murder."

"Hired by whom?"

"By Nancy Webster," Ethel said. "And what I've just told you he can prove without a doubt. I promise you that."

It was impossible to ignore the absolute certainty in her voice. "All right," Danzig said, "why do you think he might be in trouble?"

"He's been talking to everyone in town who was in any way connected with the Barrow case. It's possible he talked to the murderer himself. And if the murderer is aware of what Mr. O'Hara has discovered . . . well, that thought is what frightens me."

"Yes, I can see that it would."

"The reason I'm particularly concerned right now is that Mr. O'Hara promised me he would be at my house at five o'clock exactly to tell me of any further developments.

When he didn't arrive I made phone calls; no one seems to have seen him since he left the Daggett house late this afternoon. Please, Chief, don't think I am an hysterical woman, rushing to the police because a man is a little late for an appointment. It's the circumstances that alarm me."

"Of course." The Chief drew his phone toward him. "I think Mr. O'Hara would have reported this breakthrough and his immediate plans to his agency. Do you know which one it is?"

She shook her head. "Only that it's in Boston."

"Nancy Webster would know, of course."

"She is the only one who would. You see, no one—not even David—was aware that she had hired an investigator."

On the other phone Jimmy Corto was asking still another of the caretakers to help find Amy Lambert.

The flashlight stood upended on the storage room floor while Andy fed them. He had unbound Nancy's hands first, let her sit on the edge of the mattress to eat the sandwich he had made and drink a glass of milk. Then he taped her wrists again, and it was Amy's turn.

Her hands freed, eating and drinking, she said, "So, mean old Andy Fisher, tonight you're going to get your money, and what do you think you'll do with all that money?"

"Eat your supper," Andy said. "Hurry up."

Amy took another bite, another gulp from her glass of milk. "You going to spend it on your rabbits, Andy? Crazy old Andy, he's going to spend all that money on his crazy old rabbits!"

Even in the dim light Nancy could see Andy's face turn a mottled red. Angry, threatening, he said, "I told you, I told you be quiet. So you be quiet!"

Amy drank the last of her milk. "You hear that, Nancy? Andy's going to spend all his money on his rabbits! He's going to buy them fur coats! And big earrings for their big, big ears! And he's going to take them on a trip around the—"

Andy, shaking with mute rage, clenched his hands into fists and advanced upon the taunting child.

"Amy!" Nancy breathed a warning. "Amy, careful—"

"Andy and his bunnies," Amy singsonged, laughing, "funny Andy's funny, funny, funny bunnies—"

Her chant became an agonized scream as Andy, with a furious move, kicked her viciously. His heavy, thick-soled shoe crashed against her ankle so hard it sent her sprawling the length of the mattress. After that first awful sound Amy lay so still that Nancy thought she had fainted. She watched, sickened by her own helplessness, as Andy retaped the girl's wrists; then, still furious, he snatched up the flashlight and slammed out of the room. She heard the key turn in the lock, the sound of his steps on the stairway and then, outside, the gravel crunch and spew under his truck's tires.

She felt Amy stirring beside her.

"I did it," she said, pain and triumph mingling in her voice. "I made him so mad he forgot to take our milk glasses!"

"That's right!" Nancy said. "Amy, you did do it!"

"We can break them, Nancy," Amy said. "And we can cut ourselves loose, and then we'll get out of here."

"Amy! My God, Amy, you're terrific!"

The phone rang several times before Sabra MacWilliams heard it. Late in the afternoon, at David's insistence, she had gone up to her room to rest. "When Nancy gets home, she's going to need you," David had said. "Please,

179

for her sake, get some rest."

She knew that sleep was an impossibility but she had dutifully stretched out on her bed, and when the phone awakened her she was surprised to find that the room was dark. It was nighttime. She switched on a table lamp, slipped into her shoes, and crossed the room to her desk where the phone was still ringing. Glancing out the window she could see by the glow of the street light that her car was no longer parked outside the house. Of course— David is using it, she thought. He would have answered the phone on the first ring had he been home. He may have gone to pay the ransom. Perhaps, dear God, it was David calling to say that it was all over, Nancy was safe....

With trembling fingers she lifted the phone.

"Hello, Mrs. MacWilliam. Chief Danzig here. I'd like to speak to Mrs. Webster, please."

"I—I'm sorry, Chief. Nancy's sleeping. I wouldn't want to wake her."

"I'm afraid you'll have to, Mrs. MacWilliams. This is a police matter. She will have to be disturbed."

"You don't understand!" Mrs. MacWilliams fought the panic rising in her voice. "Nancy is ill, too ill to come to the phone."

"It will only take a minute, Mrs. MacWilliams. Believe me, it is an absolute necessity that I speak to her, or I wouldn't insist."

"I can't let you. I can't!" Panic did take over then. It was a long moment before she was able to say, "Just this morning Dr. Rankin ordered very strongly that she must not be disturbed, not for any reason."

"Dr. Rankin?"

"Yes. I'm going to have to hang up now; I must see to Nancy."

The Chief heard the click of the receiver. He hung up too.

What in hell, he said to himself, is going on over there? Dr. Jared Rankin, he knew, had been off-island, at a medical convention in Baltimore, for almost a week.

In his corner of the room, Jimmy Corto was nearing the end of his list of caretakers. So far, it being around dinner time, he had found all but three of them at home.

In the winter dinnertime was a quiet hour in Edgartown, and Main Street, as David drove down it, was almost deserted. The theatre was dark, the only brightly lighted windows were in the liquor store at the corner and, across from it, the pharmacy, in front of which he parked. He picked up the black briefcase and, concealing it under the raincoat he carried, he walked around the corner to the town's only bar open the year round.

There were just a half-dozen drinkers scattered around the saloon, and David knew none of them. He sat at the far end of the long bar; the bartender served him a double Scotch on the rocks and went back to his *Cape Cod Times*.

David looked at his watch, checked it with the clock above the doorway. Nearly an hour before he would go into the theatre and deliver the ransom. After that, what? How long before a kidnapper would pick it up? How long before Nancy would be released? If the kidnapper kept his promise, and released her.

Jimmy Corto rang the bell of the Webster house for the third time. This time he leaned against it and finally the door was slowly, reluctantly, opened. A pale, drawn Sabra MacWilliams stood facing him.

"Jimmy," she said. "What do you want, why—"

"What do I want, why am I here? Let me come in, please, and I'll tell you."   ·

181

She stepped back, gave way to the young policeman, then shut the door behind him. She leaned against it for a moment, eyes closed, before she turned to him.

"Jimmy, I told Chief Danzig that Nancy—"

"I know what you told him. Now listen to me, Mrs. Mac. Nancy hired a detective to investigate Jim Barrow's murder. Did you know that?"

"No. No, I didn't."

"That's what I've got to talk to her about. Now let me see her. If she can't come down, I'll go up—" He stopped when he saw the stricken look on Sabra's face. He said, "She isn't here, is she? Where is she, Mrs. Mac?"

She stood looking at him mutely, shaking her head from side to side, and swiftly the pieces fitted together in Jimmy's mind and made sense. The car left all night on Clam Bay, the other tire tracks and footprints near it, David's call requesting an immediate meeting, which he canceled abruptly when the rain storm broke. Rain would have erased all the tire tracks and footprints in the sand. "She was kidnapped, wasn't she, Mrs. Mac?"

"Oh, dear God, David trusted me to keep the police, or anyone else, from finding out. If anything goes wrong because of me—"

"Mrs. Mac, believe me. I promise you nothing will go wrong. Tell me what you know."

Silently, painfully, Sabra MacWilliams came to her decision. "She was kidnapped on Thursday. David got the phone call Thursday night, at eight forty. It came from Pocasset, on the Cape."

"You're sure of that?"

"Yes, because it was a collect call."

"David talked to the kidnapper?"

"No, to Nancy. The kidnapper had her do the talking. She told David the ransom would be one hundred thousand dollars. He went to Boston yesterday and got it."

"How was it to be paid? When?"

"I don't know. David thought it would be better for me if I knew nothing about the instructions. He only told me that if the kidnapper kept his word, Nancy would be home sometime tonight."

"You mean," Jimmy Corto said, "that David is out somewhere right now, paying the ransom? Right now?"

"I don't know. I told you—"

"But you think so, is that right?"

"Yes," Mrs. MacWilliams said. "The money was in the library, in a black briefcase. I looked there a few minutes ago. It was gone."

There was a long, strained silence. Then Mrs. Mac said, "There isn't anything you can do now, is there?"

"I'm afraid it's too late."

"I'm sorry, Jimmy. David thought—we both thought that if we did what we were told, Nancy might . . . she might have the best chance."

"I understand, Mrs. Mac," Jimmy said.

But damn it to hell, he thought on his way back to headquarters, he did not understand. David and Mrs. Mac have known since Thursday night, they've had forty-eight hours. If only we could have had those forty-eight hours. And the F.B.I.—the thousands of hours spent on training their agents, the millions of dollars spent on equipment, the labs, the technology—and David tries to handle it himself.

Well, maybe, he thought, God willing, maybe it would work, and Nancy would be returned safely. But then again, in this age of terrorism, he hadn't much hope.

As he told Mrs. Mac, there was nothing they could do now about Nancy. But what they had on their hands, and could and must do something about, was a missing child, and a possibly missing private investigator.

The huge gold hands on the church tower clock were indicating seven thirty when Andy Fisher parked his pickup in front of the county courthouse and, hands in pockets, walking slowly so that he limped not at all, made his way down Main Street. Across from the still dark theatre, in front of a summer restaurant, a few of the town's young Saturday night loiterers had already gathered. Lolling against the waist-high white fence that in summertime bordered a sidewalk café, they greeted him with benign amusement.

"Well, look who's here!" one of them said. "Andy Fisher, of all people! I never thought I'd see him around here on a Saturday night, did you, Bob?"

"Hell, no!" the youth named Bob said. "What the hell are you doing here tonight, Andy?"

"Hey, Bob, watch your language around Andy."

Andy smiled. They knew he always went to the movies on Saturday night, everybody knew that. He knew they were just teasing him, but he didn't mind. It was all in good fun.

"Thought I'd take in the picture show," Andy told them, going along with their fun. "That's what I'm doing here tonight."

"Is it any good?" another boy asked. "The show tonight?"

"Very good," Andy said. "I've seen it before and it's very good."

The boys, finished with Andy now, turned away to greet and tease some high school girls, and Andy, waiting for David Webster to deliver the ransom, watched a typical winter Saturday night unfold on the town's main street. Cars began coming, but not many—there were still lots of parking spaces left in back of the post office and on the side streets. Groups of people were gathering before the theatre, anxious for it to open because it was cold.

184

The wind, blowing in off the harbor and up Main Street, was strong and raw; the dead vines and flowers in the café's flower boxes crackled and rattled as it passed through them. A man and a woman went into the drug store, there were occasional customers across the street buying liquor. More boys joined the loiterers in front of the restaurant; they laughed and joked and called out to the passersby. The youngsters didn't seem to notice the cold.

Andy kept his eyes on the theatre, waiting.

CHAPTER TWENTY-THREE

*A*T TWENTY MINUTES to eight David paid for his two drinks, and with the briefcase concealed under his raincoat, he left the bar. He met no one he knew between the bar and the theatre. The theatre was now lighted and its doors were open. People were climbing the twin staircases that led to the outside second-floor landing. David went up the steps, bought a ticket, made his way to the men's room. He found it empty.

The kidnapper was someone, David thought, well acquainted with the movie house's rest room. Beneath the two sinks was a trash container easily large enough to contain the briefcase. There were paper towels on an old-fashioned roller. The trash can was empty. Without knowing why, David ripped a few feet of toweling off the roll and squashed it down into the bottom of the trash can, as though to make a nest for the ransom money. The door of the men's room opened and a blond teen-ager came in.

David turned on the cold water tap, the only one, and began washing his hands. The boy ignored the urinal, the sinks, and David. He was interested only in the mirror above the sinks. Evidently it told him that his hair needed instant attention; he gave it that. Using a barber's comb, he primped, and fluffed it, then, coiffed to his satisfaction, he went out, never so much as glancing at David.

Immediately David placed the briefcase on the nest of towels. Then he quickly piled enough additional towels on top to completely hide it from view.

The auditorium was surprisingly well filled for such a wintry night. Most of the people, he saw at a glance, were youngsters, but in the last row on an aisle seat he saw Andy Fisher, and a few rows in front of him were Tony Marcos, the deckhand, and his wife. From the other side of the theatre Mickey and Warren Jamison waved to him and indicated some empty seats beside them, but he smiled and shook his head and made his way to the third row. It was entirely empty. He sat in a middle seat.

It was seven fifty-five, five minutes before the picture was to start. The darkened theatre was filled with canned music, sentimental old tunes, while the screen was silently and quaintly reflecting advertising slides for island businesses. A local florist was urging the audience to say it with their flowers; the pitches of a jeweler, a dress shop, an island insurance company followed. Then a restaurant in Vineyard Haven, where the sale of liquor was prohibited, suggested that when you came to dine you B.Y.O.B. The restaurant had been using that same ad for years, ever since he and Nancy were kids. He remembered how amused they had been when they learned what it meant. Bring Your Own Booze. They had adopted a variant of it as a part of their language, driving their parents to distraction with their apparently meaningless and endless strings of initials. H.A.T.I.A.M.T. meant How About Taking In A Movie Tonight? Their most ambitious one, which neither of them understood, but which they thought sounded witty, was D.L.N.B.Y.F.S.I.S.: Don't Look Now But Your Freudian Slip Is Showing. And, in a sort of reverse game, the first letters of words had become a code to them. Nice And Neat—Nan—had meant Nancy for young David. Drive A Volvo Everywhere had translated "David" for her.

The last of the ads disappeared from the screen; the sweet, jazzy music stopped. The music that now pulsed into the auditorium came from a modern sound track of a Hollywood composer's score, and on the screen giant spotlights streaming through a dazzled sky announced a Twentieth Century-Fox Production.

He was tingling with excitement when he stepped out of the theatre and started down the steps to the street. It had been so easy. The men's room had been empty, he had pushed aside the crushed towels in the trash basket, and there lay the beautiful black briefcase. In a second he had slipped it under his bulky sweater. He could feel it there now, ever so comforting; security for his future. The money to buy his very own nursery.

Walking fast, not caring at all that he was limping badly, he crossed the street and made his way down to the courthouse, and climbed into his pickup. It was almost over now, he thought. In a little while it would be over. He switched on the ignition, and the lights, and shoved the gear shift into first when there was a pounding on the far window and a voice shouted, "Hey, Andy! Hey, there!"

He turned and saw it was Fred Nelson. "Hey, Andy," Fred was calling, "I want to talk to you!"

Andy leaned over and rolled down the window, but just a few inches. "I'm in an awful hurry, Fred—"

"Listen, this will only take a minute. What the hell did you really have under your tarp the other night?"

"Like I told you, Fred, I had rabbits."

"Like hell you did! You wouldn't tie your rabbits up and throw them under a tarp. Hiding them; Yeah, sure. All of a sudden you ashamed of your rabbits? Come on, Andy, what were you up to? You can tell me."

Andy stepped on the gas and yanked the steering wheel to the right. Fred leaped back to avoid being sideswiped; he stumbled backward and went sprawling in the street. He got to his feet and stared furiously after the fast-moving truck.

"Why, the little shit," he said aloud. "That simple-minded little shit. He thinks he can do that to me, does he?" Stepping up onto the sidewalk, he went quickly to the corner where there was an outside booth.

Still furious, he entered the booth, deposited a dime, and dialed Information. He asked for the Hyannisport number of Luther "Buzz" Campbell, who sold not only puppies, kittens, and hamsters but also rabbits.

The picture had been running for three, maybe four minutes when the truth hit David, hit him so hard that he jerked bolt upright, almost leaping to his feet. He knew now what Nancy had been trying to tell him, she had been playing the childhood game that he had just remembered. Everything she had said over the phone about his delivering the ransom to the theatre, telling him to remain until the end of the picture, to sit in the middle of the third row—all that had been the kidnapper's instructions. What she was secretly saying to him were the four words she kept repeating, pretending he hadn't heard her—*and now do you? And now do you?* The initials of those words spelled *Andy.*

He remembered the motel woman in Pocasset who thought the man she saw was drunk, because he staggered. But it was Andy she saw, whose walk became a stagger when he hurried.

189

Andy Fisher had kidnapped Nancy, and ten minutes ago he had been sitting in this theatre, in the last row on the aisle.

Striding up the aisle, David saw that the seat was empty now. Outside, at the railing of the outside stair landing, he desperately searched Main Street, and then directly below him saw Andy's blue pickup. By the time it turned onto Water Street, David was in his car, and in less than a minute, only thirty yards behind it.

When the blue pickup turned off on the road to Katama, David knew he was too close. Andy would realize he was being followed. He slowed, and when the truck reached a fork in the road there was a hundred yards between them. Andy took the left branch that led to South Beach, David the right that would pass the small private landing field. Immediately he stopped the car, switched off the lights, and swerved into a turnabout.

Seconds later he was back on the Katama road, driving in the dark, using the glowing tail light ahead of him as a guide. Slowly creeping up on it. But it was still far ahead of him when it turned off the road and disappeared. Driving blindly now, he managed to find the dirt road Andy had taken. He turned into it and braked to a stop. The road ahead of him forked, and on neither one was there the glimmer of a light or the sound of a motor. He had lost Andy Fisher. There was nothing before him but blackness and silence.

David groaned. He knew Katama well. Not far in the distance the road would split again into mere lanes, each leading to a summer house deep in the pine woods, or on the cliffs that abutted Katama Bay. There were five or six houses here, all of them isolated on these hundred or more acres, all of them closed at this time of year. In one of them Andy Fisher was holding Nancy.

After making his call to Hyannisport, Fred Nelson had been about to put another dime in the coin slot and make a second call, when he had a better idea. Pulling the door open, he stepped out onto the sidewalk and began walking briskly up Main Street.

They were still laboriously trying to cut the tapes on their wrists with pieces of broken glass when they heard the truck. It did not go as usual to the back of the old carriage house. It stopped in the driveway and Andy's footsteps clattered into the downstairs hall.

Nancy held her breath, waiting for him to climb the stairs. He had been to the theatre by now, he had picked up the ransom. Now it would be only a matter of minutes before it was over.

Still there was no sound of Andy on the stairway. He was moving about the first floor, from one room to another, but shunning the stairs. Then to her cautious, incredulous surprise, she and Amy were given a reprieve. Andy had gone out to his truck and driven away.

Working desperately with the glass shard, she felt the tapes at her wrists give way. In a moment she had freed her legs. On her hands and knees she crawled to Amy's side to cut her free.

That was when she smelled the smoke.

Jimmy Corto was back at headquarters, manning his phone. The Chief was at his desk. The officers in the four patrol cars searching for Amy Lambert had been calling in; all the closed houses on Clam Bay and the airport road had been covered, Al Potter had finished with the ones on Starbuck Neck, and no trace of the missing girl had been found. Four of the enlisted caretakers had reported; the houses in their charge had been searched and found empty. Now Bud Larkins, the Oak Bluffs officer, was calling in.

"I'm out on Beach Road, Chief. This house is all dark now, but when I drove in I think I saw a gleam of light, like a flashlight moving around. I'm going to go in and make sure."

"Let me know," the Chief said. "And good luck."

"Right," Bud said.

"Bud Larkins may have something," Chief Danzig told Jimmy. "A house on Beach Road."

A few minutes later, before Larkins had called back, the station door burst open. Fred Nelson, face glowing from the cold, eyes glistening with excitement, strode into the room. "Hi, Chief," he said. "Hi, Jimmy. Say, I got something to tell you fellows."

"Fred," the Chief said, "to put it mildly, we're sort of busy around here tonight. If what you have to tell us is your latest practical joke . . . well, frankly, get the hell out of here!"

"No, nothing like that," Fred said.

The radio receiver squawked.

It was Bud Larkins, from the Fielding house on Beach Road. A nephew of theirs and this girl spending the night without permission.

"Okay, Bud, cover the rest of the places there." To Jimmy Corto, the Chief said, "Maybe after we find Amy Lambert I should send Bud back to make a fornication arrest."

"Listen, Chief," Fred Nelson said. "This thing I got to tell you—"

The Chief turned to him. "You still here?"

"This thing I got to tell you could be important."

"I'll give you one minute to prove it," the Chief said.

"Okay," Fred said. "You know Andy Fisher?"

"Yes," Danzig said, and thought, good God, Andy Fisher's name coming up again tonight. "What about him?"

"The other night on the ferry from Woods Hole Andy's truck stalled and we had to push him off. I noticed something moving under the tarp in back. Andy said it was rabbits, but like hell it was rabbits. Andy wouldn't treat them like that. And what was he so nervous about? He like to faint when I ask him what was under the tarp. So I called Hyannisport and found out he hadn't bought any rabbits for months!"

"My God!" the Chief said, getting to his feet. "Jimmy, you hear this?"

"Yes!" Jimmy had left his desk and was crossing the room. "What night was this, Fred?"

"Thursday night."

"What ferry?"

"The last one," Fred said. "Ten thirty."

"Good God!" the Chief said. "When did the call from Pocasset come, Jimmy?"

"Twenty minutes to nine," Jimmy said. "Hell, yes! That's it—Andy Fisher!"

"Where's that list of Andy's empty houses?"

"On my desk," Jimmy said.

There had been no blue pickup truck near any of the three empty houses David had already been to. Having retraced his route, he was now back near the Katama road; there were only the Findlay and the Goldsmith houses to which Andy could have gone. He chose the Goldsmith road, his car jouncing wildly over the rutted lane.

The big old house loomed up like a blacked-out castle on its bluff above the sea. The driveway, the lawns beyond the house were empty. David got out of his car and ran to the carriage house, and found it empty, too.

Turning back he saw a flicker of light in a downstairs window of the big house. Then the whole window turned orange as a drapery behind it caught fire. Racing toward the veranda, he saw smoke curling out of the other windows.

The front door was unlocked. He yanked it open and smoke billowed into his face. The rooms on each side of the center hallway were on fire. He shouted Nancy's name and heard her answer from someplace upstairs.

He ducked low, under the worst of the smoke, and finding the stairway, he followed Nancy's voice upstairs until he reached a doorway halfway down the hall. He kicked it in. Wisps of smoke followed him as he plunged into the room where Nancy was standing and Amy Lambert huddled on a mattress on the floor.

"I think her leg is broken," Nancy said.

David scooped the child up in his arms and carried her into the hall, Nancy close at his heels. But then her legs, weak and stiff from disuse, failed her. She stumbled and fell to her knees. By the time she had regained her footing David was out of sight, hidden by a cloud of smoke. She had groped her way to the staircase, when sheets of flame burst through the smoke. She heard David shouting at her from below, "Go back! Go back!" warning her off the stairs.

She turned back, away from the enveloping heat, and found her way through the smoke, away from the spreading flames, to the stairway that led to the attic. The air there was like a furnace blast, and curls of smoke rose from the floor, but it had not yet caught fire. The flight of shallow steps, almost as steep as a ladder, rose to a trap door in the roof. Quaking, she mounted them, pushed open the door, climbed through it, and found herself on the widow's walk.

Fire now licked at the ladder, reaching for her; she slammed the door shut on it. Below the widow's walk the roof was in three levels, each one lower than the next; the lowest only one story high. The fire had not reached them yet and she saw her escape route. She climbed over the bannister.

On the beach road, halfway to the next summer house, Andy parked his truck in a wooded grove, and made his way back on foot to the Goldsmith house. Already he could see the spreading flames and their reflection in the water of the bay; he could smell the burning shrubs. Before long the fire alarm would sound in town, sending out the location of the blaze. Andy broke into a run. When the volunteer firemen arrived he wanted to be there to help them, the conscientious caretaker fighting to save one of the houses in his charge. No fault of his that it would be beyond saving.

As he came out of the woods he saw that the fire was spreading even more wildly than he had expected it would; it had reached the second floor and was bursting out the windows. The window of the room where he had left Nancy Ryan was in flames.

And then he saw her. High up on the roof of the house, she was climbing over the railing of the widow's walk. She was crawling along the peak of the roof toward one of the wings where the fire had not spread.

With a sob of rage and frustration, his knife in his hand, he raced across the lawn toward the blazing house.

Every patrol car engaged in the search for Amy Lambert had been deployed to one of the houses where Andy Fisher worked as caretaker; in one of those houses Nancy Webster was being held prisoner. Car number three of the Edgartown police, with Chief Danzig at the wheel and Jimmy Corto riding gun, was speeding toward Katama. Andy serviced two houses in that area; the Goldsmiths' and the Dawsons'.

"The Lambert girl," Jimmy said. "When we find Nancy, that's where we'll find Amy."

"Right," the Chief said.

The car squealed around a bend in the road and ahead of them, on the bay side, they saw a tower of flame shoot up into the dark sky.

The Goldsmith house was situated just about there.

Amy Lambert lay on the far edge of the Goldsmith lawn where David had left her before he raced back to the house. She couldn't see him now because of the smoke. But a change of wind cleared the smoke from the roof and she saw Nancy hanging from the edge, then dropping to the one below.

And it was going to be all right, Amy saw it was all right, for suddenly David was there just behind Nancy, he was making his way to her. Amy thought a little prayer of thanksgiving.

Then the widow's walk burst into flames, making everything as clear as day, and she saw that it was not David, it was Andy Fisher on the roof.

Now she could see David. He had climbed up from the roof below. But Andy had already reached Nancy, the knife glittering in his hand.

Then she saw him suddenly drop the knife; his body convulsed, and then went limp and slid off the roof like an old rag doll. Standing on the lawn not far away, she saw Chief Danzig and Jimmy Corto, and Jimmy had a rifle in his hands.

Amy looked back up to the roof. David was beside Nancy, he was holding her in his arms. Amy said another prayer of thanks. Her friend Nancy was safe.